PENGUIN  CLASSICS

UTOPIA

THOMAS MORE was born a Londoner in 1478, the son of a successful lawyer. He served as a page in the household of Cardinal Morton, who sent him on to study at Oxford. Summoned by his father to legal studies in London, he was called to the Bar from Lincoln's Inn in 1501. He had a precocious career in the City, acting for the Mercers' Company, sitting in Parliament, and becoming Undersheriff. Sent on an embassy to Flanders in 1515, he began *Utopia* there and completed it back in London. He became a privy councillor of Henry VIII in 1518 and was elected Speaker of the Commons in 1523; six years later he succeeded Cardinal Wolsey as Lord Chancellor, becoming the tenth layman to hold that office. From 1528 he actively resisted innovation in religious matters, writing works against Luther and Tyndale, among others, and sought to restrict the spread of heresy. Henry VIII's estrangement from Rome on account of his desire to divorce Catherine of Aragon increasingly put More's position under pressure and he resigned as Chancellor in 1532, although he remained involved in controversy. Required in 1534 to take the oath of succession, which rejected Papal jurisdiction and the validity of Henry's marriage to Catherine, he declined and was sent to the Tower of London. During his imprisonment he wrote a number of spiritual works, among them *A Dialogue of Comfort against Tribulation*, one of his finest writings. In July 1535, after he refused to accept the royal supremacy over the Church, he was tried as a traitor at Westminster Hall and beheaded on Tower Hill. His death caused shock abroad, especially among his fellow humanists. Adopted by the Catholic Counter-Reformation as an exemplary figure, he was canonized by Pope Pius XI in 1935.

DOMINIC BAKER-SMITH graduated from Trinity College, Cambridge. After teaching in Canada he returned to Cambridge where he was a Fellow of Fitzwilliam College and Lecturer in the Faculty of English. In 1976 he became Professor of English at University College, Cardiff, and then moved to the University of

Amsterdam in 1981 where he is now Emeritus Professor. In addition to various publications on English and Neo-Latin literature he is the author of *More's 'Utopia'* (1991, 2000) and has edited three volumes in the Toronto *Collected Works of Erasmus*. He has served as Chairman of the Society for Renaissance Studies and was appointed OBE in 1999.

THOMAS MORE

Utopia

Translated, edited and introduced by
DOMINIC BAKER-SMITH

PENGUIN BOOKS

PENGUIN CLASSICS

Published by the Penguin Group
Penguin Books Ltd, 80 Strand, London WC2R ORL, England
Penguin Group (USA) Inc., 375 Hudson Street, New York, New York 10014, USA
Penguin Group (Canada), 90 Eglinton Avenue East, Suite 700, Toronto, Ontario, Canada M4P 2Y3
(a division of Pearson Penguin Canada Inc.)
Penguin Ireland, 25 St Stephen's Green, Dublin 2, Ireland (a division of Penguin Books Ltd)
Penguin Group (Australia), 250 Camberwell Road,
Camberwell, Victoria 3124, Australia (a division of Pearson Australia Group Pty Ltd)
Penguin Books India Pvt Ltd, 11 Community Centre, Panchsheel Park,
New Delhi – 110 017, India
Penguin Group (NZ), 67 Apollo Drive, Rosedale, Auckland 0632, New Zealand
(a division of Pearson New Zealand Ltd)
Penguin Books (South Africa) (Pty) Ltd, 24 Sturdee Avenue,
Rosebank, Johannesburg 2196, South Africa

Penguin Books Ltd, Registered Offices: 80 Strand, London WC2R ORL, England

www.penguin.com

This translation first published in Penguin Classics 2012

004

Copyright © Dominic Baker-Smith, 2012
All rights reserved

The moral right of the translator and editor has been asserted

Set in Postscript Adobe Sabon
Typeset by Firstsource Solutions Ltd
Printed in Great Britain by Clays Ltd, St Ives plc

ISBN: 978-0-141-44232-7

www.greenpenguin.co.uk

Contents

Chronology

1478 7 February: Thomas born in Milk Street, Cripplegate, London, eldest son of John More, then a barrister, and his wife Agnes.

c. **1482–90** Attends St Anthony's School, Threadneedle Street.

1485 22 August: Battle of Bosworth: King Richard III killed; Henry Tudor succeeds as Henry VII.

c. **1490–92** Serves as a page in the household of Cardinal Morton, Archbishop of Canterbury and Lord Chancellor.

c. **1492–4** At Oxford, possibly at St Mary's Hall. In October 1492 Columbus lands on San Salvador.

c. **1494** Commences law studies at New Inn; admitted to Lincoln's Inn in 1496.

c. **1497** Latin verses printed in John Holt's *Lac puerorum*. In June John Cabot reaches Newfoundland.

1499 Meets Erasmus on his first visit to England; takes him to visit the royal children at Eltham Palace. Around this time More lodges in or near the London Charterhouse.

1501 Qualifies as a barrister; pursues Greek studies with William Grocyn and Thomas Linacre; gives lectures on St Augustine's *City of God* at the church of St Lawrence Jewry.

1503 Writes 'A rueful lamentation' on the death of Henry VII's Queen Elizabeth.

1504 Marries Joanna Colt and resides at the Old Barge, Bucklersbury; possible date for his first entry to Parliament. Amerigo Vespucci's fourth voyage (in April he leaves 24 Portuguese sailors at Cape Frio in Brazil, the supposed occasion of Raphael Hythloday's journey to Utopia).

1505–6 Erasmus stays at the Old Barge and collaborates with More in translating writings by the Greek author Lucian into Latin.

1509 Death of Henry VII and accession of Henry VIII; More's commemorative verses on the coronation are presented to the king. In October Erasmus arrives from Italy and completes *The Praise of Folly* (dedicated to More) in More's house.

1510 Becomes a member for London in the new Parliament and is appointed Undersheriff of the City; about this time his *The Life of John Picus* (Giovanni Pico della Mirandola, 1463–94) is published.

1511 Death of his wife Joanna; marries Alice, widow of John Middleton, merchant of the Calais Staple.

1513 Henry VIII invades France and captures Thérouanne and Tournai. Around this time More begins work on *Richard III*, in Latin and English, and continues to *c.* 1519, leaving it unfinished. In Florence Machiavelli writes *The Prince* (published in 1532).

1515 May–October, travels to Bruges as a member of a delegation to review trading terms; during a break in negotiations he meets Peter Giles in Antwerp and begins work on *Utopia*. At Bruges in October he writes the *Letter to Martin Dorp* in defence of Erasmus and of literary studies.

1516 Completes *Utopia* in London and sends manuscript to Erasmus in September; the first edition appears in December, printed by Thierry Martens in Louvain.

1517 Evil May Day riots in London against foreigners; More is instrumental in controlling the disturbances. Erasmus sends More portraits of himself and Peter Giles painted by Quentin Metsys. Paris edition of *Utopia* published, which includes More's second letter to Giles, and a letter from the French humanist Guillaume Budé. In Wittenberg Luther publishes his ninety-five theses, initiating the Reformation.

1518 Admitted to the King's Council and serves as royal secretary; writes his *Letter to the University of Oxford* supporting Greek studies. The third and fourth editions of

Utopia are printed at Basel by Froben, together with More's Latin *Epigrams*.

1519 Writes the *Letter to Lee* and *Letter to a Monk*, both defending Erasmus' edition of the New Testament and humanist studies.

1520 May–June: attends Henry VIII at his meeting with Francis I at the Field of the Cloth of Gold.

1521 Knighted and appointed Under-Treasurer of the Exchequer; enlisted to edit Henry VIII's *Defence of the Seven Sacraments* against Luther.

1523 Elected Speaker of the House of Commons; publishes his *Answer to Luther*.

1524 High Steward of Oxford University; purchases estate at Chelsea.

1525 High Steward of Cambridge University; appointed Chancellor of the Duchy of Lancaster.

1526 Conducts a visitation of the Steelyard, depot of the Hansa merchants, and seizes Lutheran books; assists Henry VIII in writing *Letter in Reply to Martin Luther*. The artist Hans Holbein stays in More's house.

1527 Rome sacked by Charles V's Imperial army in May; *c.* October, More first consulted about the possibility of a royal divorce.

1528 Licensed by Bishop Tunstall of London to read heretical books in order to defend orthodoxy.

1529 Publishes *A Dialogue concerning Heresies*; succeeds Wolsey as Lord Chancellor in October and opens the 'Reformation' Parliament.

1532 First part of *The Confutation of Tyndale's Answer* published (the second part appears early in 1533). 15 May: Submission of the Clergy; More resigns the Chancellorship the following day, claiming poor health, but remains active in religious controversy.

1533 Henry VIII marries Anne Boleyn; in June More declines to attend her coronation.

1534 30 March: Act of Succession; 13 April: More, while willing to accept the succession (of Anne Boleyn's children), refuses to take the specified oath; 17 April: sent to the Tower. Between this date and July 1535 he writes the *Treatise on the Passion*, *A Dialogue of Comfort against Tribulation*, *De tristitia Christi* and other devotional works.

1535   1 July: tried and condemned as a traitor in Westminster Hall; 6 July: beheaded on Tower Hill.

1551   English translation, *A fruteful and pleasaunt work of the newe yle called Utopia*, by Ralph Robinson.

1557   More's *Workes*, 'in the Englyshe tonge', edited by More's nephew William Rastell, published in London, with a preface addressed to Mary I.

1565   More's complete Latin works printed in Louvain, overseen by Catholic exiles linked to his own circle.

Introduction

Any reader undertaking the journey to *Utopia* will need to stay alert: few works of fiction offer to establish a more conniving relationship with those who turn their pages. This is not to suggest that reading it is a daunting experience – far from it – but rather that we have to remain open to conflicting voices and perspectives within the work if we are to recognize what Thomas More's fiction sets out to achieve. Debate and dialogue, the interplay of contrasting viewpoints, are key forms in the repertoire of humanism, and they are basic to More's achievement as a writer. In the earliest account of his life, that by his son-in-law William Roper, we are told about his precocious behaviour as a page in Cardinal Morton's household when he would jump on the stage during the performance of an interlude or entertainment 'and never studying for the matter, make a part of his own there presently among them'.[1] This spontaneous sense of performance remained with him throughout his life and found its conclusion in the dramatic statement of his death on the scaffold. This is not to suggest that More was guilty of insincerity, but simply that he instinctively related himself to an audience. So it is no surprise that his most effective literary works take the form of dialogue, a drama of ideas in which lines of thought present themselves as roles or potential courses of action.

More was, of course, celebrated for his wit, though this was not always held to his credit. The chronicler Edward Hall puts the case succinctly: 'His wit was fine, and full of imaginations, by reason whereof he was too much given to mocking, which was to his gravity a great blemish.'[2] The fact is that More's wit, his play of mind, is essentially ironic, deriving from the discrepancy between the brute facts of life and the illusions we may cherish about it. One of his simplest Latin epigrams illustrates the point: 'He is dreaming who thinks that in this life he is rich; when death awakes him he sees at once how poor he is.'[3] In the background we are clearly intended to recall Christ's parable of the complacent rich man and his well-stocked barns, 'But God said to him, "You fool, this very night you must surrender your life."'[4] On the one hand there is the voice of God, the intrusion of reality, and on the other the human capacity for self-delusion. More's wit is never just a sense of play or bare mockery; it is always directed at someone or something in order to expose folly. The full force of such irony is displayed in More's account of the fall of Lord Hastings in *Richard III*, with its sonorous conclusion, 'O good God, the blindness of our mortal nature! When he most feared, he was in good surety; when he reckoned himself surest, he lost his life, and that within two hours after.'[5] For a moment the voice of the moralist breaks into the historical narrative. This is the fundamental irony of the human condition, which any preacher might exploit; what gave More's irony its particular force was his encounter with the satirical essays and dialogues of Lucian of Samosata (born *c.* AD 120).

More had probably begun his Greek studies during his time at Oxford University but he persisted in them even after he had been recalled to London and his legal studies. When the Dutch humanist and theologian Erasmus (1469?–1536) first visited England in 1499 he was clearly impressed by More, and a shared interest in Greek may have contributed to their friendship. But it was during Erasmus' second visit in 1505 that this flowered into a collaboration to translate dialogues by the Greek ironist into Latin. In all likelihood they worked from the Greek edition printed in 1503 by Aldus Manutius, whose editions of classical authors, as Raphael tells us, were to prove so popular with the Utopians (p. 89). Out of their joint efforts came a volume of Latin translations which was published in Paris in 1506. For both authors this encounter with Lucian was to prove singularly fruitful. From him they learned the possibilities of satirical dialogue and the use of literary diversion as a social weapon. There was the additional attraction that Lucian's favourite targets, bogus philosophers and hypocritical ascetics, matched conveniently with the conservative academics and clergy who opposed the advance of humanism (and in particular Greek studies) as well as Erasmus' efforts to reanimate Christian practice.

Among the Lucianic devices that More adopts one can include his playful construction of outlandish names: Utopia itself, 'No-place', and the river Anyder, 'Waterless', are part of his Lucianic evocation of an unavailable world. But the most significant insight that he, and Erasmus, derive from Lucian is the recognition that society is founded on custom, on the unreflective adoption of received habits, whether these relate to modes of conduct or perception. One might almost say that Lucian taught them to be anthropologists. Accordingly, when Raphael comes to describe the Utopians' contempt for gold and their embarrassing ways of storing it, he adopts a hesitant tone for fear that we won't believe him: 'For it's almost invariably the case that the further removed something is from the common practice of the listeners, so much the harder is it for them to credit it' (p. 75). We are products of our customs.

The most truly Lucianic moment in *Utopia* is Raphael's account of the Anemolian ambassadors, who aim to impress the austerely dressed Utopians by the magnificence of their attire; accordingly, in addition to their cloth of gold garments, they wear chains of gold, rings and gems, oblivious to the negative connotations these carry for the Utopians. Inevitably, given the cultural assumptions of the Utopians, the Anemolians are treated with contempt; as Raphael observes, 'Just how customs so at variance with those of other nations can generate different attitudes has never struck me more forcibly' (p. 76). It's worth reflecting that when More wrote this section he was himself an ambassador and probably wore a gold chain when required. Certainly, it doesn't seem too much to suggest that More's instinctive irony was heightened into a medium for social reform by his encounter with Lucian.

The first major work to emerge from this Lucianic experience was Erasmus' *The Praise of Folly*, which he completed at More's house in 1509 and dedicated to him. More's opportunity would come later: in the meantime he was a very busy man. There is every reason to suppose that the frantic round of obligation that he describes in the first of the prefatory letters to *Utopia* addressed to his friend Peter Giles, the Flemish humanist and magistrate of Antwerp, was close to the truth. More was a prominent figure in City affairs, serving it both as an MP and as Undersheriff, the latter a time-consuming office which involved presiding over the Sheriff's court. His legal career had developed very much within the City community, and this gave him direct experience of the tensions and challenges of ordering a community of some fifty-thousand people. London was unique in England for its size and for its corporate independence, which made it comparable to major continental mercantile centres. So it is no accident that Utopian life is essentially urban and centred around civic interests, even to the extent that there appears to be no overriding central authority to run the country. When More and Peter Giles meet in Antwerp it is as the representatives of a distinctly civic culture.

Utopia was the outcome of unexpected leisure. As More reveals at the opening of the book, when a commission was set up in May 1515 to negotiate with the representatives of Charles of Habsburg, he was among its members. While the diplomat and churchman Cuthbert Tunstall was the political leader, More was included to voice City interests since the 'matters that were far from trifling', as he calls them (p. 23), related to English trade with the Netherlands. The delegation arrived in Bruges on 17 May, and discussions continued until late July, when the Flemish negotiators were recalled in order to consult with Prince Charles in Brussels. So More now enjoyed a period of diplomatic inactivity which he seems to have used to the full. For a start he went to Antwerp to stay with Peter Giles, and this was followed by visits to Mechelen, where he admired Jerome Busleyden's collection of antique coins, and to Tournai, then in English hands. But, as he later wrote to Erasmus, 'in all my travels I had no greater good fortune than the society of Peter Giles',[6] and it is there, in the thriving port of Antwerp, that we can place the conception of *Utopia* or, to give it its proper name, *On the best state of a commonwealth*.

More remained in the Netherlands until October; his last act there was to complete his *Letter to Martin Dorp*, his most comprehensive and forceful defence of humanism and of his friend Erasmus. By the end of the month he was back in London. What meanwhile had happened with *Utopia*? It would be more than a year before the book was published, so what can we conjecture about its hidden life?

Utopia falls naturally into two parts: it is dominated by Raphael's account of the extraordinary island which he visited on his travels, so dominated in fact that people sometimes discuss the work as if it consisted simply of Book Two. But there is, of course, Book One and the fictional setting that it provides – the conversation in an Antwerp garden which may be less vivid but is crucial in focusing our attitude towards Raphael and his remarkable account.

It may be helpful to think of the book in terms of three concentric circles: at the centre of the fiction is Raphael's description of Utopia and its customs and institutions, but that is set within the frame of the conversation in the garden of More's lodgings in Antwerp, and then that in its turn is enclosed within the prefatory materials – the Utopian alphabet and verses and the various letters. These mark three distinct phases in the composition of the work, and equally three stages in its imaginative conception. These were persuasively outlined by J. H. Hexter in his study *More's Utopia: The Biography of an Idea* (1952), but the first hint was given by Erasmus himself when he reported that 'the second book [More] had written earlier, when at leisure; at a later opportunity he added the first in the heat of the moment'.[7] Presumably 'the heat of the moment' refers to the hectic life that More resumed after his return to London: Erasmus' friend Andrea Ammonio, the king's Latin secretary, reports of More's return, 'he haunts those smoky palace fires in my company. None bids my lord of York good morrow earlier than he.'[8] 'My lord of York' was Wolsey, newly elevated to cardinal, and the fact that More was haunting the palace shows that he was increasingly being drawn into government business.

The idea that *Utopia* reflects More's personal dilemma at the prospect of a royal invitation may be overstated, but clearly he faced a career shift from the institutional stability of the City to the less predictable theatre of court politics, even if he did not finally enter the Council until March 1518. He had, after all, made a careful study of the classical historians, especially Tacitus and Sallust, and his semi-humorous allusion in *Utopia* to the clash between the Emperor Nero and his counsellor Seneca in the tragedy *Octavia* shows that he knew all too well the frustrations and dangers of advising the powerful (p. 49). So it's hardly surprising that he decided to dramatize the issues and incorporate them into his tentative work on the best state of a commonwealth. In any case we can take it that the comical self-portrait that he gives in his initial prefatory letter to Peter Giles is close to the truth: that the only time that he could find for writing was 'whatever I can filch from sleep or food' (p. 12).

The second phase of composition may well have been done in a sudden creative burst: Erasmus visited England very briefly in the August of 1516, but there would have been time for More to discuss his manuscript with him and bring it to a conclusion. The fact that Erasmus left in late August and More then sent the manuscript after him a few days later suggests that there were a few loose ends to tie up. At this stage More still calls his work *Nusquama*, 'nowhere'. The first mention of 'Utopia' occurs in a letter from the Dutch humanist Gerhard Geldenhouwer to Erasmus in November, reporting that the book will shortly be published by the Louvain printer Thierry Martens. It duly appeared in the following month.

All this indicates that More wanted his book to seen as part of a wider European cultural movement, one aiming at the promotion of classical literature and in particular Greek studies.[9] Just the sort of interests, in fact, that are pursued by the Utopians in their leisure hours. Leaving aside Ralph Robinson's English translation of 1551, the first printing in England of More's Latin text appeared at Oxford as late as 1663. More conceived the work in the course of his travels in the Netherlands and he entrusted its publication to his friends there, the most active support coming from Erasmus and from Peter

Giles. Did Erasmus devise the name Utopia? That we can't tell
with any certainty, but Giles claims responsibility for the notes
in the margin, the Utopian alphabet, and for those verses in
Utopian 'which Hythloday showed to me after More had left'
(p. 17). All the indications are that More used his protracted
stay in the Netherlands to extend his literary contacts, and that
Utopia and the prefatory letters are the most obvious outcome
of these. But there is also that polemical letter to Martin Dorp,[10]
which offers us an insight into More's preoccupations at the
time. It is a defence of Erasmus but, more importantly, of the
intellectual programme he stood for, which is conventionally
presented under the label of humanism.

The *Letter to Dorp* takes its place in a swathe of anti-scho-
lastic polemics that runs roughly from Petrarch's *On His Own
Ignorance* (*c.* 1371) to John Milton's *Areopagitica* (1644).
While humanism was intimately bound up with the revival of
classical learning and literature, at its centre was a sense of
language as a social medium. It would be unwise to take the
humanist attacks on scholasticism at face value, but they did
have a point: the scholastic emphasis on language as a severely
technical medium, deliberately stripped of subjective reference,
set up a barrier between learning and everyday life. Although
the medieval achievement in philosophy and theology was
formidable, it increasingly failed to connect with ordinary
experience. The humanist appeal to rhetoric, the classical art of
persuasion, was based on its ambition to link study and reflection to practical action; instead of being confined to specialized
debate between initiates, Latin could function as a medium for
transforming life. This, basically, is the theme of More's repri-
mand to Dorp.

In the *Letter* More distinguishes between narrow academics
'who know nothing at all outside a tangled labyrinth of petty
problems' and those, like Erasmus himself, who are not unaware
of technical issues but possess something much more useful, 'a
general command of sound literature'.[11] This too, we find, is
the basis of the Utopian curriculum: the majority of citizens
devote those hours of leisure which are a unique feature of
Utopian life to the study of 'good letters' (p. 78), which is not

to say just poetry or drama or fictional narratives but equally works of history or moral philosophy; everything, that is, which can extend their understanding of human existence. Raphael is presenting the Utopians as good humanists when he reports, 'While they equal the ancients in most things, they fall far short of the inventions of our modern logicians' (p. 79).

To equal the ancients is to share in a common human culture, but to equal the moderns is to become trapped in a closed system of sterile speculation. Utopian education is designed in the first place to produce good citizens: it is overseen by the priests (who, we should remember, are few in number and consequently worthy of their role) and they take care to instil in the minds of the young 'principles that benefit the life of the community' (p. 113). As Raphael emphasizes, the state of a commonwealth is directly affected by the kind of attitudes that its members absorb in early life. But education doesn't end there, since most Utopians extend it through those optional lectures which fill their spare time. To More's contemporary readers these would have been one of the most astonishing features of Utopian life. Rather than working towards some restricted professional competence, such higher education aims to fulfil those aspirations which are common to all humanity, moving through contemplation of the natural world to a sense of awe in the face of its maker.

In one of Lucian's more fantastic travel tales, which ironically he calls *A True History*, his narrator lands on the Isles of the Blest where he comes face to face with great figures from the past. One notable figure is missing, however, and that is Plato, who is allegedly living in his imaginary city under the constitution and laws that he drew up himself.[12] Lucian's joke is directed at the impossibility of Plato's ideal society, and it must be alluding to a particular moment in the *Republic* when Socrates brings up the issue of political action: to put it simply, will the wise man participate in public life or retain his independence? He must choose between two 'cities' or communities: that of actuality, the 'world of his birth' as Socrates puts it, and that of an ideal community, a city which is placed in words and can be found 'nowhere on earth'.[13] It's easy enough to see why

Lucian makes the idealist Plato invisible, but there is a serious issue involved too: what is the role of imagination, the faculty which liberates us from our immediate environment, in the practical issues of conventional life? How can we relate our disturbing ability to picture alternative worlds to the inherited world into which we have been born? One option, as Socrates makes clear, is to remain faithful to the ideal and keep out of practical politics. The other, implicitly, is to compromise, and risk moral pollution in consequence. It is this issue of political engagement that forms the underlying theme of *Utopia*.

In a Lucianic spirit More approaches the serious topics playfully; as the title declares, it is a book 'no less instructive than delightful'. When *Utopia* appeared from the press of Thierry Martens it included several features designed to disconcert the literal-minded. On the title-page there is the serious statement of intent, a discussion of the best state of a commonwealth, but this is linked to the topical mention of a newly discovered island and all that that suggested in 1516, while the author reveals himself as Undersheriff of London. Then, in order to authenticate the book's claim to be a travel account we are given a map, the Utopian alphabet and specimen verses in Utopian. So far as we can tell, these were added by Peter Giles and other collaborators, but clearly they are part of the conspiracy to confuse fiction with the real thing. Just how far Giles shared in the project is clear from his prefatory letter, addressed to Jerome Busleyden. There were in fact several prefatory letters and verses, and these were added to in later printings, but just three stand out as extensions of the fiction, two by More himself and the one by Peter Giles, and these are the ones included in this translation. Readers tend to skip prefatory letters, and often they have good reason, but in the case of *Utopia* it needs to be stressed that they are integral to More's conception.

One thing that the reader should be aware of from the outset is the distinction between the author himself, identified on the title-page as Undersheriff of London, and his fictional self, the 'More' who engages in dispute with Raphael. It's important to consider these figures separately, so we can refer to the fictional

self by his Latin name, Morus. The figure that passes as More
in his two letters to Peter Giles has many features in common
with Thomas More, the busy lawyer with scarcely a moment in
which to write, but his earnest concern with historical accuracy
identifies him as Morus. There is an air of Chaucerian self-
deprecation about this portrait: he is apologetic about the delay
in completing the work since his role has been an entirely pas-
sive one; no eloquence, no invention was called for: all he had
to do was act as a conduit for Raphael's narration. Hence
his anxiety about the bridge at Amaurot and its precise length
(pp. 12–13); the book must have nothing untrue in it, it must
mirror the 'reality' which Raphael has witnessed. Then Giles's
letter plays further with the theme of fiction, with *seeing* the
unreal: you can tell from Raphael's words that he has *seen* what
he is talking about – in comparison to him the fêted Amerigo
Vespucci[14] seems to have seen nothing. And yet, Giles cannot
avoid the sense that there is more to be seen in More's report
than Raphael saw in his five years in Utopia. Inevitably, as we
are about to learn the location of an island that is 'nowhere',
a coughing fit drowns out the information. The third letter, again
from More to Giles, allows Morus to meet the charge that the
book may be made up and to defend its authenticity, 'even if
historical objectivity had not compelled me, I'm not so dense
that I would have chosen such outlandish names as Utopia,
Anyder, Amaurot or Ademus, which signify nothing' (p. 20).
And that, thanks to their negative prefixes, is just what they do
signify (see Glossary of Names, p. 131).

Apart from providing some Lucianic entertainment to
More's humanist circle, these prefatory letters function as
pointers to the reader. They prepare us for the text that is to
follow and alert us to its element of play, but as so often with
play, they nudge us in the direction of more serious issues. In
particular they thrust at us the problematic relationship between
imagined worlds and mundane reality, using the metaphor of a
traveller's tale to represent the traffic between the two. This is
the aspect of *Utopia* brought out in the alphabet and those
prefatory verses which Giles appears to have added to More's
manuscript: that Plato's commonwealth is merely philosophical

while Utopia is presented to us as a living environment, a place that we can vicariously inhabit. One purpose of fiction is, after all, to generate encounters with the ideal. It is striking, then, that at the opening of the book we are thrust into a very specific context with all the features of actual 'history'. We hear of an embassy that did occur, we read the names of real persons who took part in the negotiations, and when Morus and Giles meet it is after Mass at the cathedral at Antwerp. All this evokes a world that is verifiable. But when the carelessly dressed Raphael is introduced a new dimension opens up: for one thing his rather scruffy appearance matches Lucian's Cynic in one of the dialogues More had translated: 'my long hair and my dress are so effective that they enable me to live a quiet life doing what I want to do and keeping the company of my choice'.[15] And then there is the name and its rather disconcerting implications: 'Raphael' may be the name of an archangel, a heavenly physician, but 'Hythloday' is ambiguous: the one certain element is *hythlos*, nonsense in Greek, and that, some had argued, is just what Socrates speaks.[16] His credentials leave us rather in the air.

It seems likely that More wrote the opening pages, those which deal with Raphael's travels, as a prelude to the actual account of Utopia, but just as we encounter the first mention of the Utopians he appears to change course and insert the dialogue about political engagement which frames Raphael's monologue on the islanders and their way of life. The shift is made with some ingenuity: Raphael's intriguing account of his travels prompts Peter Giles to suggest that he enter the service of some king, thus setting off the debate about participation in public life which is one of the major strands in the book. Raphael treasures his independence; he lives as he pleases, while Morus enters the conversation in order to argue the case for royal service. This proves to be a critical confrontation.

Although the book is set in Antwerp, and for the most part in the garden of More's lodgings, we are scarcely aware of this since for much of the time we are whisked off on imaginary journeys. Almost the whole of Book Two is given over to Raphael's evocation of the Utopian world; but in Book One there is a sequence of episodes, starting with Raphael's recall of Cardinal Morton's household and proceeding to the fly-on-the-wall views of two royal councils at work, each episode containing an appeal to some exemplary alternative – the Polylerites, the Achorians and the Macarians. The glue that binds these episodes together is a running argument over political participation. The two court scenes, for all their precise focus on contemporary events, are relatively straightforward, but the Morton episode is more complex. It is introduced by Raphael to support his case that the court environment is resistant to change, and he dates his English visit by reference to the Cornish uprising of 1497. This may seem an odd event to pick, but it leads logically to the themes of economic hardship and social injustice which will colour the whole passage. Indeed, there are stylistic parallels between this section and Raphael's peroration at the close of Book Two in which he condemns the existing order as a conspiracy of the rich. The two sections may have been written at much the same time, in the last stages of composition, and they both convey deep anger.

Years later, as Chancellor, More would have occasion to clash with his fellow common lawyers over too literal a reading of the law, and now in the setting of Morton's house it is the common lawyer who sets off the dispute over hanging. Simply, Raphael considers hanging for theft too extreme. As he protests, 'nothing that's subject to fortune can be weighed against the value of a human life' (p. 36). An equitable system of reformatory justice, like that practised by the Polylerites, offers a better alternative. There is a deeper point as well, that theft is not just a private act but reveals a social problem: the thief steals out of necessity since he must feed his starving family but has been deprived of any legitimate means of earning a livelihood because the rich have other plans for the countryside. So the guilt for the theft is dispersed throughout society; even abbots are driven by the profit motive.

It would be difficult not to be impressed by Raphael's metaphor of man-eating sheep (p. 33). The trend towards enclosure (whereby landlords converted arable land to pasture, usually for sheep farming and often with a resultant loss of common rights) may have peaked in the late fifteenth century, but the problem remained an issue in 1516, accentuated by a series of bad harvests; in May 1517, six months after the publication of *Utopia*, Wolsey set up a commission to look into depopulation and enclosure. In any case, from his seat in the Sheriff's court, More must have seen at first hand the social tragedies of a displaced population. The real point, however, is not how accurately he mirrors the social conditions of the day, but rather how fully he grasps the way in which crime can be socially predetermined. There may be a hint of early rural nostalgia in Raphael's call to restore agriculture, but More's real insight is the recognition of what some would describe as social sin, the awkward fact that to belong to society – to be formed by its customs and to be subject to its dictates – is to be morally compromised. As a simple illustration we have the hangers-on at Morton's table, from the common lawyer himself to the crowd who flatter the cardinal at every opportunity. In them moral vision is confined to personal advantage or the upholding of custom. By contrast Morton, who is open to innovation and willing to consider Raphael's proposal, emerges as a positive figure who anticipates the adaptability of the Utopians themselves. Within the closed circuit of social custom his readiness to assess the penal arrangements of the Polylerites offers a glimpse of hope; one can even see it as an example of counsel achieving its goal. But does Raphael notice?

As the conversation in the garden unfolds, a key issue is the relationship between wisdom, or philosophy, and power. If wisdom is to reform society it needs the backing of power. Plato's ideal solution, invoked by Morus, is the concept of a philosopher-king, one in whom power and philosophy coincide. No polity can achieve perfection until, under divine providence, either philosophers take power or the powerful develop a passion for philosophy.[17] But in the absence of such an improbable coincidence, Morus argues, the philosopher can at least try to advise whoever exercises power. The problem, of course, is custom, that accretion of received attitudes and practices which distorts the way we see things, as in the case of gold. Raphael's retort is that those in power have been corrupted by false values since infancy, and to confirm his claim he delivers the two accounts of royal councils in session. These have been devised with some care: the imaginary scene of the French royal council is based on the dominant features of French diplomacy between the Battle of Marignano in September 1515 and the death of Ferdinand of Aragon in the following January. It's a vivid exposition of pragmatism and territorial ambition. The second council is tactfully unspecified, but it closely matches the fiscal policies pursued by Henry VII and his notorious councillors Empsom and Dudley.[18] Were Raphael to intervene and present the alternative values of the Achorians or the Macarians, he would encounter a highly negative reaction, as Morus concedes.

But Morus' point is about context: short of a perfect world, you must adapt to circumstance and avoid head-on confrontation; otherwise you will risk derision or worse. Instead he advocates an 'indirect approach', a tactful attempt to modify the evil effects of custom, 'so that whatever you cannot turn to good will at least do the minimum of harm' (p. 50). It amounts to a containing exercise, a policy for the interim until all men become good; and that, as he wryly puts it, is unlikely for some time. Again these contrasted philosophies amount to different modes of language: on the one hand there is Raphael's direct and unaccommodating speech, which makes no condescension to particular circumstance and which Morus characterizes as 'academic' (p. 49), the language of theory; on the other hand there is Morus' own more nuanced approach, one that adapts to the setting and is *civilior*, more urbane and attuned to public affairs.

It is this urbane philosophy that connects with the humanist tradition and its sense of language as a means to action. In the absence of a philosopher-king the best we can do, according to Morus, is try to persuade the powerful to act philosophically. But this implies engaging with a less than perfect society, soiling one's hands in effect, and that Raphael refuses to consider: he is committed to a world of absolute justice, and he has no wish to compromise. Like Socrates in Plato's *Republic* he is a citizen of the ideal. Behind More's fictional dialogue lies an ancient debate that had a personal resonance for him, that of contemplation *versus* action. One of its most widely known formulations is found in Cicero's *De officiis* (*Of Duties*) where he considers those, like Raphael, who place the pursuit of truth before civic obligation: 'For they secure one sort of justice, to be sure, in that they do no positive wrong to anyone, but they fall into the opposite injustice; for hampered by their pursuit of learning they leave to their fate those whom they ought to defend.'[19] What More confronts us with is a clash between two concepts of justice: while Raphael follows Plato's austere idealism, the course proposed by Morus is clearly Ciceronian, asserting a moral obligation to engage in civil life. In his view there can be little hope for society when philosophers refuse to counsel those in power. But to Raphael such engagement is futile since society, that conspiracy of the rich, is impervious to high-minded interventions, a point he illustrates by the example of Christ's teaching, which has been watered down by preachers to fit ordinary behaviour. In just the same way, he argues, the arrangements that Plato *imagines* in his republic or that the Utopians *practise* in theirs seem absurd to us because we hold to private ownership, while there all is held in common. So this key issue is brought out into the open: Raphael is convinced that 'the one and only way to social well-being is equality of possessions' (p. 52), while Morus counters with the conventional Aristotelian-scholastic arguments for private property. So forceful is Raphael's claim that Book One ends with Morus' invitation to describe this remarkable island and its way of life.

Before we move on to consider the Utopians and quite what they represent, it's important to notice how the rude inhabitants of Abraxa with their mud huts have been transformed into cultivated city-dwelling Utopians. The whole pattern of their society can be traced back to Utopus, the conqueror who seized the island and shaped it to his own conception. In him we can see a philosopher-king who embodies the coincidence of power and philosophy. Not only is he responsible for the layout of the towns and for freedom of religious observance, but he caused the excavation of the broad channel which separates what is now an island from the neighbouring continent. Like so many fictional societies Utopia is almost inaccessible to the outside world, and in consequence its institutions and the attitudes they promote can operate without contamination. But, apart from this channel, what else divides Utopia from other societies? The most obvious answer is its communism, or – to put it better – its community of goods: this is its defining feature. So what did More have in mind? For anyone who reached maturity at the opening of the sixteenth century two things might prompt reflection on contemporary society. One was the inherited corpus of classical literature, now foregrounded by the impact of humanism; the other was the information brought back by travellers about the natives of the New World. Both helped to stir an interest in primitivism, in the origins of human traditions – an interest that More and Erasmus shared in common.

When he discusses the proverb that opens the 1515 edition of the *Adages*, 'Between friends all is common',[20] Erasmus attributes it to the semi-mythical figure Pythagoras, who reputedly founded a community in which all things were shared. But his most striking reference to Pythagoras comes in another of the 1515 adages, his attack on militarism, 'War is sweet to the uninitiated'.[21] There, in a passage adapted from Ovid, Pythagoras traces the origins of war to the human slaughter of animals for food. Erasmus is not advocating a vegetable diet, but he is making a symbolic point about the cycle of degeneration from a state of natural simplicity 'when the first primitive men lived in the forests, naked, without fortifications or homes', down to the battlefields of Renaissance Europe.[22] Such simplicity was noticed also among the natives of Cuba: as one traveller reported, 'with them the earth, like the sun and water, is common, nor do "mine and yours", the seeds of all evils, fall among them'.[23] The Utopians live in splendid cities and they do some work, even if they don't toil like European peasants; but clearly they mark an alternative line of development from the one which has produced Renaissance Europe. Thanks to Utopus they have evolved from the primitive state of nature without elaborating a culture based on property rights – that would be the legacy of Rome to Europe.

Book One is dominated by property issues, whether land rights as in the Morton episode or dynastic claims as in the French council, and these culminate at the very close of *Utopia* in the conspiracy of the rich that so enrages Raphael: 'Once the rich, in the name of the community (and that, of course, includes the poor), have decreed that these fraudulent practices are to observed, they become laws' (p. 120). The shift from a state of nature to private ownership is summarized by Cicero in his *De officiis*: 'There is no such thing as private ownership established by nature, but property becomes private either through long occupancy or through conquest or by due process of law, bargain, or purchase, or by allotment.' Put that way, it doesn't sound a very tidy process. Cicero is anxious to add, in the spirit of Plato, that we have an obligation to contribute to the general good, but in a sense the horse has already bolted. Lip service is paid to those things which have been produced by nature for the common good, provided they don't encroach on the rights of private property.[24] The whole process by which natural law is subordinated to civil law and to private interests is what the Utopians have evaded, thanks to the intervention of Utopus. To the listeners in Antwerp Utopia suggests an alternative social order which may at times seem tantalizingly within reach, but which is ultimately inaccessible.

The devotion to Greek studies which motivates More and Erasmus goes beyond the language itself; there is also the ambition to regain access to an alternative culture, whether this be to recover lost traditions of thought, or to establish a more authentic text of the New Testament. In either case Greek provides the basis for a critical review of the established order, indebted as that is to the law and values of Latin tradition, the legacy of Rome. The Utopians show a natural affinity for all things Greek because of a common radicalism that places them on the margins of European experience.[25] When it turns out that the natural theology of the Utopians provides an effective infrastructure for Christianity, one important factor is their discovery that Christ taught a common way of life to his followers, confirming as it were the

inheritance of Pythagoras. But there is little evidence of that
left in contemporary Christendom; as Erasmus sourly observes,
'never was wealth held in greater honour among pagans than
it is nowadays among Christians.'[26] The negative view of
imperial Rome which is evident in More's outlook would have
been reinforced by St Augustine's pathology of its decline in
The City of God (AD 413–26), a book that More knew well
and had lectured on in 1501. It was from Augustine that More
derived the idea of Rome as the *civitas terrena*, the city of this
world whose institutions perpetuate the transmission of injustice from generation to generation.

More's account of his new-found island is an impressive
feat of imagination, not least because of its consistency. This
derives from its appeal to nature as the basis of value: 'to live
in accord with her precepts is their idea of virtue' (p. 81). In all
areas of life the promptings of nature indicate the course to be
followed, and nature's promptings are defined as the voice of
reason, which, in its turn, is supplemented by 'certain principles drawn from religion' (p. 80), moral intuitions which act as
important social constraints. All this provides a sharp contrast
with the custom-directed world of Europe where even pleasures tend to be artificial constructs. These may provide some
form of spurious gratification for the few but they fall far short
of true happiness, *felicitas*, which is the goal of Utopian life
and which, on account of our common nature, should be available to everyone. The Utopians' manner of dress is typical of
their whole way of life, with undyed wool or linen worn over
practical leather working clothes – so natural needs are comfortably met, but without any scope for individual display.
When we picture Utopians we don't seem to see any faces, just
figures, in the same way as we encounter no Utopian names.
The whole drift of life in a Utopian city, from the common
meals to the pre-dawn lectures, is designed to meet authentic
human aspirations in a manner that excludes no one; but in
order to achieve this end both privacy and individualism have
to be suppressed. The parallel is often drawn between a Utopian city and a monastery: the resemblance lies in the way
both institutions subordinate personal concerns to a common

goal, which entailed, as Plato recognized, the elimination of ownership.[27]

Faced by the Utopian polity and its many positive features, the modern reader may find some others rather puzzling. For one thing, there are slaves in Utopia, though their status is never inherited but imposed as a penalty for crime. There are, of course, those foreigners who willingly become slaves there, largely to underline the point that slavery in Utopia is better than poverty elsewhere, and these must be the *famuli* or bondsmen who act as butchers and do other more demeaning tasks. But the majority of the slaves are paying the penalty for breaches of the rational code which governs social life. Prisoners of war, specifically those captured fighting the Utopians themselves rather than their allies, are also enslaved, and for much the same reason – that they have opposed a rational and just cause. Generally, one could say, More's real concern is to portray a penal system which benefits society and rehabilitates prisoners rather than providing a supplementary labour force.

Much the same emphasis on rationality also colours Utopian relations to other lands. Should the population rise above the prescribed maximum, they establish colonies on the mainland wherever there is unused or neglected land. The natives of the area are encouraged to participate as equals in developing it, but if they refuse they are driven out. Some have seen this as evidence of More's 'colonialism', but it has to be set against Raphael's point that the Utopians see themselves as 'cultivators of the soil rather than its exploiters' (p. 58). Their aim is to realize the full potential of whatever nature provides. So in much the same spirit they undertake wars of 'liberation' to release subject peoples from tyranny: the basis of their policy is to promote the rule of reason, to preserve their own rational way of life and where appropriate to extend it to others. In this respect they seem to follow close on Plato's distinction between wars of Greeks on Greeks (who also see themselves as rational beings) and wars of Greeks on barbarians.[28] When it comes to the actual waging of war, however, the remorseless objectivity of Utopian methods provides an ironic contrast with the

delusions of contemporary chivalry. War is vile, is the implication, and if you are drawn into it the aim must be to end it as
swiftly as possible. Against this harsh realism one needs to set
the example of the Utopian priests whose role on campaign is
to keep bloodshed on both sides to the minimum and to curb
the ferocity of the victors.

Utopia's reputation as a work of political idealism has meant
that all too often More's analysis of what is wrong with the real
world has been overlooked. Once Raphael has finished his
survey of Utopian life and institutions he concludes with a
short but searing account of the 'ungrateful society' (p. 120) all
too familiar to his listeners. While Utopia is a true commonwealth which provides security for all, regardless of their
condition, Europe shows all the calamitous effects of divorcing
conventional values from natural ones. Private ownership
together with the subversive effects of a money economy combine to establish domination by the few and all the bogus values
of an aristocratic culture driven by display and consumption.
As with the Morton episode in Book One, it is impossible to
miss the notes of anger and compassion which resonate through
the writing. But at this point Raphael moves beyond issues of
social injustice to introduce a moral concept, pride, this 'serpent
from hell' (p. 121), which blocks access to a better way of life.
In *The City of God*, the work that More lectured on as a young
lawyer, St Augustine identifies pride or self-love as the primal
sin, the driving force behind the earthly city, the world as we
experience it. Raphael may rejoice that the Utopians have
achieved their commonwealth and have somehow escaped from
the common condition of humanity, but he seems less than
hopeful that their example can be imitated: 'pride is too deeply
embedded in human nature to be easily torn out' (p. 121). For
all his enthusiasm he leaves us with a distinctly negative prospect; like Lucian's invisible Plato he is an alien in our world.

When Morus and Raphael argue in Book One about the role
of counsel in public life, it is Morus who tries to adapt to the
actual conditions of a world governed by pride: it is, as he says,
inconceivable that all will go well until all men become good,
'and that I don't anticipate for quite some time to come' (p. 50).

After the force of Raphael's intervention, Morus may seem an anti-climactic figure: he is sensible, unromantic, perhaps (as the letter to Giles suggests) rather unimaginative. His role is to reassert normality, to remind us that we are in Antwerp, not Utopia, and so he finds many Utopian practices absurd, not least that 'linchpin of their entire social order', the absence of money. As he solemnly concludes, 'This one thing by itself utterly subverts all nobility, magnificence, splendour and majesty, which according to popular opinion are the proper ornaments and honours of the commonwealth' (p. 122). Knowing More (as opposed to Morus), it is hard not to sense irony in the reference to 'popular opinion', and yet that almost heraldic list of qualities has its validity. It may present the polar opposite of Raphael's anonymous commonwealth, but a line of thought running through Aristotle to Thomas Aquinas and beyond would accept the social role of the wealthy man and see his philanthropy and patronage as works of magnanimity and even spiritual virtue. This is the world in which More the ambassador is operating.

So at the end the dialogue offers no clear-cut resolution, instead the issues are thrown out at us, the readers. Raphael may offer the excitements, and indulgences, of a radical stance, but Morus' pragmatic accommodation to things as they are, his modest ambition to make things a little less bad, has its own vindication. There is even the sense that at the close he has modified his position – perhaps he cannot accept all that Raphael has described, but there are those features in Utopian life which he could wish to see 'in our own cities' (p. 122), however unlikely the prospects may appear. He has become a little infected by the ideal, and surely this is the point: that More wrote a dialogue because he did not want to exclude either voice; they are in a sense interdependent. Indeed, both are visible in the pattern of his own life, at first within the arena of public life as he endeavours to make things less bad, and then in his final phase as a resolute outsider. What the book proposes is a state of mind rather than any particular state of society, and to achieve this both voices have their contribution to make.

It is its conflicting voices that explain the resilience of
Utopia and its success in appealing to such a variety of readers, from disaffected satirists to aspiring reformers. Between
1516 and 1750 twenty-five Latin versions appeared; not a
striking number, but the popularity of the book owed far more
to the translations and adaptations which appeared across
Europe. As the universal adoption of its title indicates, it has
had a wider impact than any other Neo-Latin work. Probably
the most concrete response to Raphael's account was that of
the Mexican bishop Vasco da Quiroga, who adapted the Utopian polity for the Indian communities that he established
between 1532 and 1534. His example at least serves to illus-
trate the way in which, until relatively recent times, it was
Raphael and his rejection of the established order that captured the interest of readers, even to the extent of blotting out
Book One altogether and identifying Raphael as the voice of
More himself. As result the book becomes a prescriptive text
rather than a debate, one slanted in a republican direction.
Typical of the way in which Utopia parts company with *Utopia*
is Francesco Sansovino's survey of political systems, *Del gov-
erno dei regni et delle republiche* (Venice, 1561), where More's
imaginary state is inserted along with other actual regimes
such as Spain or Sparta. Of course, one reader who engaged
fully with the subtleties of More's Lucianic narrative was
Jonathan Swift, whose *Gulliver's Travels* (1726) pays explicit
homage to More as well as adopting his techniques, but it is
unlikely that Swift would have shared the liberal views that
were increasingly associated with the work in the Enlighten-
ment and which were projected onto More himself. The
ultimate stage in this development was the inclusion by Marx
and Engels of More's name among the founding figures of
English communism. William Morris, whose own *News from
Nowhere* (1890) contributed to the genre, likewise hailed
Utopia as 'a necessary part of a socialist's library'.[29] It was
only in the twentieth century that the wider fictional frame of
the work was brought back into focus and its reputation as a
radical manifesto qualified. Once again Morus emerged as an
alternative voice and even, as some have argued, the voice of

the author. It may seem a strange paradox that, after its initial reception, a book published in 1516 should have to wait so long for the kind of attentive reading it demands, but perhaps the really important point is that *Utopia* has been liberated from Utopianism. Instead of some imaginary blueprint for a fantastic society we can now recognize in it a searching meditation on the nature of politics.

NOTES

1. William Roper, *The Lyfe of Sir Thomas Moore, Knighte*, ed. E.V. Hitchcock (London: Oxford University Press, 1935), p. 5.
2. Edward Hall, *Henry VIII*, ed. Charles Whibley (London: T. C. & E. C. Jack, 1904), vol. 2, p. 265.
3. No. 79, in *The Complete Works of St. Thomas More* (New Haven and London: Yale University Press, 1963–97; referred to below as *CWM*), 3:2, 145.
4. Luke 12:17–21.
5. *CWM* 2, 52.
6. Letter 388, *Collected Works of Erasmus* (University of Toronto Press, 1974– ; referred to below as *CWE*), 3, 235.
7. Letter 999 to Ulrich von Hutten, *CWE* 7, 24.
8. Letter 389, *CWE* 3, 239.
9. For an illuminating account of the Greek revival, see Simon Goldhill, *Who Needs Greek? Contests in the Cultural History of Hellenism* (Cambridge University Press, 2002).
10. Martin Dorp (1485–1525), a Louvain theologian with literary interests, had expressed concern about the direction of Erasmus' writings, especially *The Praise of Folly* (1509), and his emphasis on the study of Greek.
11. *CWM* 15, 15.
12. *A True History*, in C. D. N. Costa, trans., *Lucian: Selected Dialogues* (Oxford University Press, 2005), p. 223.
13. Plato, *Republic* 592a–b; the passage has obvious relevance for More's title.
14. Amerigo Vespucci (1454–1512), the Florentine traveller after whom America was named, won fame through his somewhat unreliable accounts of his journeys to the New World.
15. *Cynicus* in *CWM* 3:1, 167; Raphael asserts, 'As things are I live as I please' (p.28).

16. The accusation of Thrasymachus, in Plato, *Republic* 336d; for an explanation of the name, see the Glossary of Names, p. 131.

17. For Plato's discussion of the issue, see *Republic* 473c–d; 499b–c.

18. The lawyers Edmund Dudley (1462?–1510) and Sir Richard Empsom (d. 1510), who were identified with the oppression of his father's reign, were imprisoned by Henry VIII immediately on his accession in 1509 and duly executed.

19. *De officiis* 1.9.28, trans. W. Miller (London and Cambridge, Mass.: Loeb Classical Library, 1961), p. 29.

20. For the text, see Appendix 1, pp. 123–125.

21. *Adages* IV.i.1, CWE 35, 399–440.

22. CWE 35, 408–10; in Utopia butchery is done by slaves since Utopians hold that it deadens the sense of compassion.

23. Peter Martyr d'Anghiera, *First Decade of the Ocean* (1511), 1.3.24. (For full text see Appendix 2, p. 127, last paragraph.) This commonplace is also cited by Erasmus in Appendix 1, and appears to be a distorted reading of Plato's *Republic* 462c.

24. Cicero, *De officiis* 1.7.21, 1.16.51.

25. For an illuminating exposition of the Greek–Roman tension, see Eric Nelson, *The Greek Tradition in Republican Thought* (Cambridge University Press, 2004).

26. *Adages* IV.i.1, CWE 35, 420.

27. Plato, *Laws* 739c; Erasmus makes the identification explicit, 'What else, I ask you, is a city than a great monastery?', Letter 858, in CWE 6, 89.

28. Plato, *Republic* 468b–471b.

29. Preface to the Kelmscott edition of *Utopia* (Hammersmith, 1893), p. iv.

Further Reading

More's Works

The complete body of More's writings has been made available in the Yale edition of *The Complete Works of St. Thomas More* (*CWM*), 15 volumes (New Haven and London: Yale University Press, 1963–97). These include introductions and commentary, with a parallel English translation of the Latin text. *Utopia*, edited by Edward Surtz SJ and J. H. Hexter, appeared as volume 4 (1965) and this provides the fullest commentary available in English, together with an introduction that has sparked off fifty years of debate. *Utopia: Latin Text and English Translation*, edited by George M. Logan, Robert M. Adams and Clarence H. Miller (Cambridge University Press, 1995), provides the most reliable Latin text and is the basis for the present translation. The standard edition of More's letters is still *The Correspondence of Sir Thomas More*, edited by E. F. Rogers (Princeton University Press, 1947), but there is a useful *Selected Letters* also edited by Rogers (New Haven and London: Yale University Press, 1961), which translates the major Latin letters.

More's Life

The two earliest *Lives*, by William Roper and by Nicholas Harpsfield, are available as a joint volume in the Everyman's Library. Peter Ackroyd's *The Life of Thomas More* (London: Chatto and Windus, 1998) places More vividly in his contemporary setting, while John Guy's brief but penetrating study

Thomas More (London: Arnold, 2000) clarifies the facts and gives a full bibliography. Biography and many other aspects are covered in two important collections of essays: *Essential Articles for the Study of Thomas More*, edited by R. S. Sylvester and G. P. Marc'hadour (Hamden, Connecticut: Archon Books, 1977), which contains a section on *Utopia*, and *The Cambridge Companion to Thomas More*, edited by George M. Logan (Cambridge University Press, 2011). The latter contains essays on aspects of More's life and his major works, as well as comprehensive bibliographical information.

Utopia

Earlier interpretations tended to focus on More's apparent advocacy of communism, and two such studies which still retain their interest are Karl Kautsky's *Thomas More and his Utopia*, translated by H. J. Stenning (London: A. & C. Black, 1927), and Russell A. Ames, *Citizen Thomas More and his Utopia* (Princeton University Press, 1949). Modern readings have stressed the inner tensions of the book, and a vivid instance is Stephen Greenblatt's *Renaissance Self-Fashioning: From More to Shakespeare* (University of Chicago Press, 1980; repr. 2005). *More's 'Utopia'* by Dominic Baker-Smith (London: HarperCollins, 1991; repr. University of Toronto Press, 2000) explores its conflicting themes, while More's engagement with classical thought is reviewed by George M. Logan, *The Meaning of More's 'Utopia'* (Princeton University Press, 1983). The implications of More's book as a critique of humanism have been analysed by Quentin Skinner in *The Foundations of Modern Political Thought*, 2 vols. (Cambridge University Press, 1978), vol. 1. pp. 255–62; in *The Cambridge History of Renaissance Philosophy* (Cambridge University Press, 1988), pp. 448–52; as well as in a seminal essay, 'Sir Thomas More's *Utopia* and the language of Renaissance humanism', in A. Pagden, ed., *The Languages of Political Theory in Early Modern Europe* (Cambridge University Press, 1987); repr., with revisions, as 'Thomas More's *Utopia* and the virtue of true nobility', in Skinner's *Visions of Politics*, 3 vols. (Cambridge University Press, 2002), vol. 2, pp. 213–44. Some important modifications to Skinner's 'neo-Roman' view are proposed by Eric Nelson in *The Greek Tradition in Republican Thought* (Cambridge University Press, 2004). The London background is discussed by Sarah Rees Jones in 'Thomas More's *Utopia* and medieval London', in Rosemary Horrox and Sarah Rees Jones, eds., *Pragmatic Utopias: Ideals and Communities, 1200–1630* (Cambridge University Press, 2001). Among more specialized studies, Andrew J. Majeske's *Equity in English Renaissance Literature: Thomas More and Edmund Spenser* (New York and London: Routledge, 2006) provides an illuminating reading from the perspective of More's legal interests. Finally, the important influence of St Augustine on More's thinking is examined by Peter I. Kaufman, *Incorrectly Political: Augustine and Thomas More* (Notre Dame, Indiana: University of Notre Dame Press, 2007). The strange afterlife of *Utopia* has been described in Terence Cave, ed., *Thomas More's 'Utopia' in Early Modern Europe* (Manchester University Press, 2008).

A Note on the Text

The Latin text used in this edition is that established by George M. Logan, Robert M. Adams and Clarence H. Miller in their *Utopia: Latin Text and English Translation* (Cambridge University Press, 1995), itself based on the Froben edition of March 1518. More dispatched the manuscript of *Utopia* to Erasmus in September 1516, together with his prefatory letter to Peter Giles. We can only conjecture what happened to it between that date and publication at Louvain in December but, if we can believe Giles, he added some verses and marginal notes, and it may well have been at this stage that the rather arbitrary section headings were inserted in Book Two.

I have retained with slight modifications the various 'outlandish' names that More devised for his Lucianic fiction, not least because they have been integral to the reception of *Utopia* over four hundred years; the reader will find a full explanation of them provided in the Glossary of Names (p.131).

UTOPIA

ON THE BEST
STATE OF A COMMONWEALTH
AND ON THE NEW ISLAND
OF UTOPIA

A truly golden handbook,
no less instructive than delightful,
by the most learned and distinguished author
THOMAS MORE,
citizen and Undersheriff of the renowned
City of London.

Map of Utopia by Ambrosius Holbein, from
the Froben edition of March 1518.

a b c d e f g h i k l m n o p q r s t u x y

ΘⲐⲪⲪⲐⲐⲐⲒⲒⲰⲰⲂΔⲓⲖ┌⸢⸤⸥◻⊟◲◻⊟⊟

TETRASTICHON VERNACVLA VTO-
PIENSIVM LINGVA.

Vtopos   ha   Boccas   peula   chama.

⊟◻ⲓⲖ┌ⲖⲂⲒ◌   ⊖Ⲗ◻ⲪⲪ◻⊟   ┌ⲒⲂⲒ◌   ⲪⲒ◌Δ◌

polta   chamaan

┌ⲖⲂⲒ◌   ⲪⲒ◌Δ◌◌Ⲗ.

Bargol   he   maglomi   baccan

⊖◌┐ⲖⲂ   ⲒⲒ   Δ◌ⲒⲂⲖΔⲰ   ⊖◌ⲪⲪ◌Ⲗ

soma   gymnosophaon

⊟ⲖΔ◌   ⲐⲒΔⲓ┐ⲂⲖ┌Ⲓ◌┐Ⲗ.

Agrama   gymnosophon   labarem

◌Ⲑ┌◌Δ◌   ⲐⲒΔⲓ┐ⲂⲖ┌ⲒⲖⲖ   ⲂⲪⲐⲪ◻ⲂΔ

bacha   bodamilomin

⊖◌Ⲫ┌◌   ⊖ⲖⲪ◌ΔⲰⲂ┐Δ⸤.

Voluala   barchin   heman   la

⊟ⲖⲂⲂ◌┐ⲪⲪ   ⊖◌◻ⲪⲪ┐⸤   ┌ⲒΔ◌⸤   ⲂⲪ

lauoluola   dramme   pagloni.

ⲂⲪ⊟ⲖⲂⲂⲖⲂⲪ   Ⲫ◻◌Δ◌⊖   ┌ⲪⲪⲂⲖⲖⲰ.

HORVM VERSVVM AD VERBVM HAEC
EST SENTENTIA.

Vtopus me dux ex non insula fecit insulam.
Vna ego terrarum omnium absq; philosophia,
Ciuitatem philosophicam expressi mortalibus.
Libenter impartio mea, non grauatim accipio meliora.

b ı

The Utopian alphabet, with a quatrain in that
language followed by a translation into Latin,
from the Froben edition of March 1518.

A Literal Translation of the Utopian Quatrain

The leader Utopus turned me from a non-island into an island. Out of all lands I alone, without abstract philosophy, have pictured for mortals the philosophical city. I share my own things freely; not unwillingly I accept things that are better.

A Six-line Stanza on the Island of Utopia
by Anemolius,[1]
Poet Laureate and Nephew to Hythloday
by his Sister

Remote, in distant times I was 'No-place',
But now I claim to rival Plato's state,[2]
Perhaps outshine it: he portrayed with words
What I uniquely demonstrate with men,
Resources, and the very best of laws.
So 'Happy-place'[3] I rightly should be called.

THOMAS MORE SENDS GREETINGS TO PETER GILES[1]

Dear Peter Giles,

I feel quite ashamed to be sending you this little book about the Utopian commonwealth after almost a year, when I'm sure that you anticipated it within six weeks. After all, you knew that I was spared the effort of devising the material and had no need to reflect on its arrangement: it was enough for me to repeat verbatim what you and I had heard Raphael say. Consequently, there was no call to strive after eloquence, seeing that his speech couldn't be polished in any case; for a start, it was off-hand and extempore, and then, as you know, the man himself is not so much at home in Latin as in Greek. The closer my language came to his casual simplicity, so much the closer would it be to authenticity, and this is the one thing that I ought to have been – and have been – concerned about in this matter.

So, my dear Peter, I admit that having all this matter to hand so reduced the burden on me that there was scarcely anything left to do. In other circumstances, either the devising or the arranging of the topic would have demanded no little time and effort, even from someone who was by no means lacking in intelligence or in learning. And if it had been a requirement to present it with as much elegance as accuracy, there is no way I could have done it, however long or hard I worked. But as it turned out, all those concerns which would have cost so much effort having been lifted off my shoulders, it only remained for me to write down in plain terms what I had heard – not too much to ask. However, my other obligations left me less than no time to attend even to this little task. Most of my day is taken up by legal affairs, so at one moment I'm pleading a case, at another I'm hearing one, then I'm settling a dispute, and at another handing down a judgement. At the same time visits must be paid to somebody out of official obligation and to someone else on business matters; almost the whole day I'm out dealing with others, and what's left I devote to my family, which leaves just nothing for myself – that is, for writing.[2]

Naturally, when I get home I have to talk with my wife and chatter with the children, as well as speak to the servants. All this activity I count as part of my duty since it has to be done (and so it does unless you want to be a stranger in your own house), and it's certainly an obligation to make yourself as pleasant as you can to those whom nature, or chance, or your own choice have made the companions of your life, provided that you don't spoil them by over-familiarity or so indulge them that you turn servants into masters. Between all these activities that I've described, the days, the months and the years slip by.

When, then, do I write? And so far I've said nothing about sleep, or even about eating for that matter, which for many takes up as much time as sleep itself, and that consumes close on half our lives. The only time that I get for myself is whatever I can filch from sleep or food, and because that is so scant things have gone slowly; but since it is at least something, I have at last finished *Utopia* and I've sent it to you, dear Peter, so that you can read it and advise me about anything that may have escaped me. For although I'm not lacking confidence in that respect (I could wish that my intelligence and learning were a match for my by no means unreliable memory), yet I'm not so confident that I believe nothing could have slipped by me. For my servant, John Clement, has thrown me into considerable uncertainty: you'll recall that he was present, since I don't want him to miss out on any discussion that might prove profitable (as one day, I hope, this young plant who is just putting out green shoots in Latin and Greek will give us a splendid harvest).[3] Now so far as I can remember, Hythloday stated that the bridge which spans the river Anyder at Amaurot was five hundred yards long; but my John says that you must subtract two hundred yards from that, as the river there is scarcely more than three hundred wide. So I ask you to review the matter in your memory. If you agree with him I'll go along with it and admit my error, but if you don't remember it, then I'll stick with the figure that I seem to recall myself. For I've taken great care to see that there is nothing untrue in the book, so that if anything is uncertain I would rather utter an untruth than tell a lie, since I prefer to be honest rather than clever.[4]

Nevertheless, it will be easy enough to remedy this if you enquire of Raphael himself either directly or by letter, and that's going to be necessary anyway because of another question which has struck me, and I'm not sure whether you or I or Raphael is more to blame. For it didn't occur either to us to ask, or to him to say, in what part of that new world Utopia may be found. I'd be prepared to pay quite a considerable sum of money to undo this particular omission: for one thing, it embarrasses me that I don't know in what ocean this island, about which I have written so much, is situated; and then, there are several among us keen to go, and one in particular, a godly man and a theologian by calling, who burns with an ardent desire to visit Utopia, not out of any empty and indulgent curiosity to witness new sights, but so that he might nurture and increase our religion, which has had such a promising start there. In order to do this in the proper manner, he has decided to petition that he might be sent there by the Pope and be appointed bishop to the Utopians. He's not inhibited by any scruples about soliciting this bishopric for himself, since he regards it as a holy ambition which is directed at piety rather than honour or advantage.

So for this reason I beg of you, dear Peter, to make contact with Hythloday – either in person, if you can manage that, or, if not, by letter – and ensure that this work of mine contains nothing that's false and omits nothing that's true. It might even be best to show him the book itself: no one is better qualified to correct any errors, but even he can't do this unless he looks over what I have written. What's more, in this way you'll be able to detect whether or not he's pleased that I've written this work. Clearly, if he has decided to commit his adventures to writing himself, he's unlikely to want me to do so; and it's certainly not my wish to snatch away the charm of novelty from his account by making the Utopian commonwealth common knowledge.

Yet, to be frank, I haven't fully settled in my mind whether I should publish it at all. People's tastes vary so widely: some have such a sour disposition, their minds are so ungrateful, their judgements so absurd, that it seems a happier prospect to go along with those who blithely indulge their own inclinations than to heap cares on one's head by publishing something useful and delightful which others will receive with either disdain or resentment. Most people are ignorant of literature, and many of them dismiss it. The boor rejects whatever isn't manifestly boorish; the pedants scorn as vulgar whatever isn't peppered with obsolete words. For some only the ancients are pleasing, and for many others only their own writings. This man is so sombre that he'll tolerate no jokes, and that one so insipid that he can't stand wit. Some people are so snub-nosed that they dread all satire just as someone bitten by a mad dog dreads water.[5] Then others are so inconstant that they applaud one thing when they're seated and quite another standing up.

Then you've got those who sit about in taverns and over their cups pass judgement on writers' abilities: solemnly, as the mood takes them, they condemn each author, dragging him down by his writings as if they'd got him by the hair. Meanwhile, they keep themselves just 'out of range' as the saying has it – so shaven and shorn are these good men, in fact, that there's not a hair left to grab them by.[6]

In addition, some people are so lacking in gratitude that even when they are delighted by a work this doesn't make them any better disposed towards the author. They're not unlike those discourteous guests who, when they have been lavishly entertained at a sumptuous banquet, set off for home stuffed, without so much as a word of thanks to the host by whom they had been invited. Off you go now, and prepare at your own cost a feast for those with such pampered palates and disparate tastes, who moreover are so full of gratitude and thanks!

But nonetheless, my dear Peter, do sort out with Hythloday the points that I've raised; afterwards it'll be in order for me to review the material once more. However, should he give his approval – since it's too late to be wise[7] now that I've finished the task of writing – and seeing that what remains all relates to publication, I shall follow the advice of my friends, and above all yours. So farewell to you, my dear Peter Giles, and also to your admirable wife. Keep me in your affection as you have been accustomed to do, since I'm fonder of you than ever.

PETER GILES OF ANTWERP SENDS GREETINGS TO THE DISTINGUISHED JEROME BUSLEYDEN,[1] PROVOST OF AIRE AND COUNCILLOR TO THE CATHOLIC KING CHARLES

My most accomplished Busleyden,

Just the other day Thomas More, one of the outstanding orna-ments of our age (as you well know from personal acquaintance), sent me his *Island of Utopia*. Thus far it's only known to a few, but it deserves to be known to all as surpassing Plato's *Republic*, all the more since it has been so clearly presented, so vividly depicted and put before our eyes by an exceptionally articulate man, that as often as I read it I seem to myself to see far more than I could through hearing Raphael Hythloday's words – for I was present at his talk, along with More. Mind you, Raphael showed no common degree of eloquence in setting out his theme, so it was easy to see that he wasn't just relating what he had picked up from the accounts of others but rather things that he had witnessed directly with his own eyes and encoun-tered over an extended period. To my mind his knowledge of lands, peoples and affairs renders him the superior of Ulysses; I can't think of any comparable figure from the last eight hun-dred years – by comparison Vespucci seems to have seen nothing.[2] Quite apart from the fact that we describe what we have seen more effectively than what we have heard about, the man had a highly individual talent for relating his experiences. All the same, as often as I reflect on these as drawn by More's pencil, I am so caught up by them that not infrequently I seem to myself to be actually living in Utopia.[3] And, heaven knows, I can't help thinking that in the five years he dwelt on that island Raphael saw less than can be seen in More's description.

In that there are so many marvels that I don't know what to wonder at first, or most: whether it should be the recall of his highly effective memory, which could repeat almost word for word so much that he had merely heard about; or else the insight by which he has exposed those sources – quite beyond the reach of popular conjecture – from which both evils and the possibilities of good arise within the body politic; or, for that matter, the force and scope of his delivery, in which, with such purity of Latin and such vigour, so many things are comprehended – and this from a man heavily taken up with public and domestic responsibilities. But all this will come as no surprise to you, most learned Busleyden, since you already know from your familiar dealings with him the superhuman and almost divine gifts he possesses.

So in all this there is really nothing that I can add to what he has written. I have simply added a quatrain in the Utopian vernacular which Hythloday showed to me after More had left, and before it I have placed their alphabet, as well as adding some little notes in the margin.[4]

Now, as to the position of the island, which so troubles More, Raphael was not wholly silent on the matter, although he touched on it lightly and in passing, as if reserving it for another place. But then, goodness knows how, some evil chance struck us both. For while Raphael was actually speaking about it, one of More's servants slipped in to whisper something in his ear; and although I listened all the more attentively, one of the party, who I suspect had caught a cold while at sea, coughed so loudly that some of the speaker's words were drowned. Truly, I shall not rest until I have fully clarified the matter and can give you not only the position of the island but also the exact elevation of the pole at that point – provided of course that our Hythloday is safe and well. For there are various rumours circulating about the man, some claiming that he died on the journey, others that he reached his homeland but then, in part because he found the habits of his countrymen intolerable and in part because he yearned for Utopia, he went back there.

As to the objection that the name of the island is not to be found in the cosmographers, Hythloday had a neat reply of his own: for it was perfectly possible, he said, that the name used by the ancients was later changed, or that the island had escaped their notice, just as today many lands are discovered that were unknown to the old geographers. But what's the point of establishing authenticity with these arguments when More himself vouches for it?

Finally, I respect his uncertainty about publication and attribute it to his modesty. But it strikes me as wholly inappropriate that the work should be delayed any longer. Indeed, it is a matter of urgency to get it into readers' hands, especially when it's commended to the world by your patronage; both because More's qualities are so well known to you, and because no one is better fitted than you to guide the commonwealth with sound counsel, a duty which you have now performed for many years, earning the highest praise for your judgement and integrity. Farewell, you Maecenas[5] of learning and glory of our time.

Antwerp, 1 November 1516

THOMAS MORE SENDS
MANY GREETINGS
TO HIS FRIEND
PETER GILES[1]

My dear Peter,

I was highly delighted with that criticism you are already familiar with, made by the sharp-witted individual who proposed
this dilemma about our Utopia: 'If it's presented as something
true, I can spot a number of absurdities in it; but if it's made up,
then I find More's sound judgement lacking in not a few of its
features.' Whoever the man is (I would guess that he's learned
and I see that he's a friend), I'm extremely grateful to him. For I
can't think of anything else that has pleased me more since the
appearance of my little book than this frank judgement of his.
For first of all, either led on by fondness for me personally or
drawn by the book itself, he appears not to have been put off by
the effort but to have read it entirely through, and not in that
rushed and perfunctory way in which priests tend to say their
office[2] (assuming they say it at all), but slowly and attentively in
order to assess each point with rigour. Then, having censured
just a few points, he declares that he approves the remainder,
and not casually but with discernment. Finally, by those very
words with which he excoriates me, he conveys far more praise
than those who have deliberately set out to applaud me. For he
shows quite clearly how generously he thinks about me when he
bitterly complains that his hopes were dashed whenever he read
something that lacked precise focus; whereas, for my part, it
would be as much as I could hope to produce at least a few
things, among so many, that weren't entirely absurd.

All the same, if I can deal as candidly with him as he has with me, I don't see why he ought to consider himself so penetrating or, in the Greek term, so 'quick-sighted', either for spotting some absurd practices among the Utopians, or for finding my ideas on the regulation of a commonwealth somewhat fuzzy: as if other nations never did anything absurd, or if, out of all those philosophers who have discussed the commonwealth, or the ruler, or the household, there ever was even one who devised things in such a way that none of his proposals had to be modified. For that matter, were it not that I hold sacred the time-honoured memory of outstanding men, I could easily extract from each of them several notions which I might confidently propose for general condemnation.

Now, it's when he wonders whether the account is true or made up that I find his own good judgement at fault. I don't deny that if I had decided to write about the commonwealth, and a tale like this had sprung to mind, then I might have settled for a fiction by which the truth could sweetly slip into the mind as though smeared with honey. But I would certainly have so ordered matters that, even though I wished to exploit the ignorance of the crowd, I should at the very least have set up signals for the more literate to alert them as to what was going on. Accordingly, if I had just applied such names to the governor, the river, the city and the island as would warn the skilful reader that the island was nowhere, the city illusory, the river waterless, and the governor without a people, it wouldn't have been difficult, and a lot more subtle than what I actually did; for even if historical objectivity had not compelled me, I'm not so dense that I would have chosen such outlandish names as Utopia, Anyder, Amaurot or Ademus, which signify nothing.[3]

On top of that, my dear Giles, I see that some people are so wary that in their vigilant wisdom they can scarcely bring themselves to credit what simple and trusting souls like us wrote down from Raphael's report. So just in case my good name and the trustworthiness of the narrative should be at risk among these people, I'm happy that I can say of my offspring what Mysis says in Terence's play about Glycerium's baby, out of fear he might be taken as a changeling: 'By Pollux! I'm grateful that there were some women of standing at his birth.'[4] And so it's turned out as well for me that Raphael told his story not only to you and me but to many other men of unimpeachable integrity and weighty judgement; I don't know whether he told them of more or of greater things, but they were certainly not fewer or lesser things than he related to us.

But if these disbelievers won't accept them either, let them go to Hythloday himself, for he's not dead as yet. Only recently I heard from some travellers coming out of Portugal that on the first of March last he was as sound and vigorous as ever. So let them enquire about the truth from him, or let them delve it out of him by questions; I simply want them to realize that I am answerable for my own work alone, and not for anyone else's reliability.

So farewell to you, my dearest Peter, as also to your delightful wife and to your lively little daughter. My wife sends her best greetings to you all.

BOOK ONE

The most invincible Henry, King of England and eighth of that name, a prince richly endowed with all the qualities of an outstanding ruler, recently had a dispute with Charles, the most serene Prince of Castile, over matters that were far from trifling,[1] and sent me as ambassador to Flanders to discuss and resolve them. I was to accompany and assist that exceptional man Cuthbert Tunstall,[2] whom the King, to general acclaim, has recently appointed Master of the Rolls. I'll say nothing in praise of him, not because I'm afraid that the testimony of a friend will carry little weight, but because his integrity and learning are too widely celebrated for it to be necessary, unless, as the proverb has it, I wished to show the sun with a lantern.[3]

Those appointed by the Prince to deal with us, all of them men of high standing, met us at Bruges as arranged. Their principal and leader was the Burgomaster of Bruges, a very striking figure. But their spokesman and guiding spirit was Georges de Themsecke, the Provost of Cassel, whose eloquence derived as much from natural flair as from training; he was deeply learned in the law and, thanks to his wit as well as long experience, a consummate negotiator. When, after several meetings, there were still various points on which we failed to agree, they took leave of us for some days and went to Brussels to consult with the Prince.

In the meantime, as my own affairs dictated, I made my way to Antwerp. Among those who visited me during my stay there, none was more welcome than Peter Giles, a native of that city, where he was much respected and already occupied high office, being fitted for the very highest; indeed, it's hard to tell whether this young man stands out more for his learning or for his moral character. For he's truly upright, exceptionally well-read and considerate to all, while to his friends he is so open-hearted, so warm, trustworthy and sincere, that you would be hard put to it to find anyone anywhere whom you might rate his equal in the attributes of friendship. He has a rare modesty; no one is less given to deceit or better combines prudence with simplicity. On top of all this, his talk is so entertaining and witty without a hint of malice that, although I had been away for more than four months, my longing to see my own country again, and with it my home, my wife and my children, was eased by his engaging company and delightful conversation.

One day I attended Mass in Notre Dame, the most handsome and frequented church in Antwerp, and after the service had ended I was preparing to return to my lodgings when I saw Peter talking with a stranger, a man verging on old age, sunburnt, with a shaggy beard and a cloak slung carelessly over his shoulder. It struck me from his face and attire that he was a ship's captain. When Peter caught sight of me he came over and greeted me. I was about to respond when he drew me aside and, pointing to the man with whom I had seen him talking, muttered, 'Do you see this character? I was just about to bring him over to you.'

'He would have been most welcome for your sake,' said I.

'But for his own too, if only you knew the man,' he answered, 'for there's no man living today who can give you such an account of unknown peoples and lands, a topic that I know you are always keen to hear about.'

'So, my guess wasn't such a bad one,' I replied, 'for at first glance I suspected that he was a ship's captain.'

'Then you are right off target,' he said, 'for he hasn't sailed like Palinurus, but rather like Ulysses, or, better still, Plato.[4] For this man, Raphael as he's called, his family name being Hythloday, is far from incompetent in Latin and is especially well versed in Greek. He studied the latter more than Latin because he's devoted himself wholly to philosophy, and he realized that in that field there's nothing of any substance in Latin apart from certain pieces by Seneca and Cicero.[5] Driven by a desire to see the world, he left to his brothers the patrimony that was his due at home (he happens to be Portuguese), attached himself to Amerigo Vespucci, and was his constant companion on the latter three of those four voyages which you now read about everywhere.[6] Except that on the last one he didn't return with him: instead he nagged and pestered Vespucci, and so far prevailed that the latter let him be one of twenty-four men who were left behind in a fort at the furthest point of that final trip. So he was left there in order to gratify his own inclination, being more taken up with his travels than his last resting place. He had the habit of remarking, "He who has no grave is covered by the sky", and "Whatever the place, it's the same distance from heaven."[7] Such an attitude might well have proved costly if God had not been gracious to him. Once Vespucci had departed, he travelled through many territories along with five companions from the fort, and at length, having arrived by a happy turn of fortune in Ceylon, he got from there to Calicut where he conveniently met up with some Portuguese ships and finally, against all expectation, regained his homeland.'

When Peter had given this account, I thanked him for his thoughtfulness in introducing me to a man whose conversation he had every reason to hope I would enjoy. I then turned to Raphael. After we had greeted each other and exchanged the usual civilities of strangers who have met for the first time, we set off for my place, and there we began to talk, seated on a turf-covered bench in the garden. He described to us how, once Vespucci had departed, he and his companions who had stayed behind in the fort began bit by bit to win the favour of the local people by familiar contact and reassuring words until they were able to live alongside them not only without danger but even on friendly terms. A certain prince – his name and that of his country have slipped my mind – also established warm relations with them. Thanks to his generosity, as Raphael told us, he and his five companions had been provided with ample provisions and means of travel, rafts by water and wagons by land. He also provided a reliable guide who could bring them to other rulers they wished to visit, and supplied them with favourable introductions. After many days of travel, Raphael said,

they encountered numerous towns and cities, and populous
states that were far from badly governed.

It is clear that under the equator and on both sides of the
line, as far as the sun's orbit extends, there lie vast deserts
scorched with perpetual heat: the entire region is harsh and
desolate, untilled and savage, inhabited by wild beasts and ser-
pents, as well as by men who are as wild as the beasts themselves
and no less dangerous. But as you travel further the landscape
gradually relents: the climate is less extreme, the earth supports
plant life and the wild creatures are milder. In time you reach
peoples and cities and settlements that are busily engaged in
trading by land and by sea, not only among themselves and
their immediate neighbours but even with distant nations. As a
result Raphael and his companions had the opportunity to visit
many lands in every direction, since no ship was made ready
for sea in which they weren't welcome aboard. He described
the ships which they saw in the first countries that they visited
as flat-bottomed and driven by sails made of stitched papyrus
or wicker-work, but later they encountered vessels with pointed
keels and canvas sails, comparable in every way to our own.
Their sailors were not unskilled in reading the waves and the
sky, but he told us of their particular gratitude to him for
instructing them in the use of the compass, something quite
unknown to them up to that time. Because of this they had
been accustomed to tackle the sea cautiously, and then only in
the summer season, but now they have such confidence in the
lodestone that they ignore the dangers of winter, and are more
reckless than safe. There is a real risk that through their lack of
forethought this instrument, which seemed to hold out such
promise for the future, may prove the cause of many evils.

Raphael's account of the sights he encountered in each place
would take an age to repeat, and in any case that's not the purpose of this work. Maybe we can deal with them on another
occasion, especially such things that it's as well not to be ignorant about – which is to say, the just and far-sighted arrangements
that he observed among those nations living together in civil
order. We questioned him eagerly about these matters, and he
answered us as willingly, leaving aside, however, the topic of

monsters since that yields nothing new. There's almost no place where you won't find Scyllas, ravening Celaenos, man-eating Laestrygones and such-like horrors,[8] but wise and well-instructed citizens you'll scarcely encounter anywhere. For the rest, just as he noted a good many faulty practices among these new-found peoples, so also he mentioned not a few which our own cities, nations, peoples and kingdoms might draw on to correct their errors. But, as I've said, I'll write about these in another place: for the moment I wish to relate only what he told us about the customs and institutions of the Utopians, while first of all presenting the discussion which prompted him to mention that republic.[9]

Now Raphael had been judiciously describing the errors found both among us and in the new world (and there are plenty of them), and he had also touched on the wiser measures adopted by both sides, so depicting the customs and institutions of each land he had passed through as if he had spent his entire life there. Peter was highly impressed. 'I wonder, my dear Raphael,' he said, 'that you don't attach yourself to some king. For I can't think of a single one by whom you wouldn't be most welcome, seeing that with your learning and your experience of places and peoples you're equipped not only to divert him but also to instruct him with examples and guide him with counsel. By the same token, you would promote your own interests and prove a support to your relatives and friends.'

'As for relatives and friends,' responded Raphael, 'I'm not too bothered, since I judge myself to have discharged my obligations to them quite adequately. All those possessions that others won't release until they are old and sick – and then only with reluctance when they can't cling on to them any more – I distributed among my relatives and friends while still fit, lively and youthful. I think that they ought be content with my generosity, and not demand or even hope that for their sakes I should enslave myself to any king.'

'Fine words,' said Peter, 'but my idea isn't that you should be in servitude to a king, but rather in service.'

'There's only one syllable of difference between the two,' snapped back Raphael.

'Well,' said Peter, 'whatever name you choose to give it, in my view it's the one way in which you can not only be useful to others, both in the private and public spheres, but also make your own lot happier.'

'Happier?' exclaimed Raphael. 'By following a course I find repugnant? As things are I live as I please,[10] and I strongly suspect few of those decked in purple manage to do that. Indeed, there are quite enough suitors for the favours of the powerful already for you not to feel deprived if they have to get along without me or one or two like me.'

At this point I cut in, 'It's clear, my dear Raphael, that you don't hanker after riches or power, and certainly I honour and respect anyone who shares your attitude no less than I do those who wield absolute power. All the same, you'll seem to act in a manner worthy of yourself and of your generous and reflective nature if you can bring yourself to apply both your intellect and your energy to public issues, even at the cost of some private inconvenience. There's no way you can do this more effectively than by entering the council of some great prince and directing him, as I know you would, towards just and honourable actions – for a stream whether of blessings or evils flows down from the prince to the people as from some unfailing spring. Your learning is so comprehensive, even without your practical experience, and your experience so extensive, even without your learning, that you would be an exceptional adviser to any prince you care to name.'

'You're mistaken twice over, my dear More,' he replied; 'first of all about me, and then about the actual situation. For I don't have the ability you attribute to me, and even if I had it to the highest degree, were I to sacrifice leisure to practical affairs, I would in no way benefit the community. After all, most princes devote themselves more willingly to the arts of war (about which I know nothing nor wish to) than to the good arts of peace; most of their effort is expended on procuring new kingdoms, by fair means or foul, rather than governing properly those they have already. What's more, you'll find no one among the councillors of kings who isn't either too wise to need advice from others, or at least thinks himself too wise to welcome it.

Apart, that is, from the fatuous sayings of the prince's favour-
ites, which they applaud and flatter in order to curry favour for
themselves. It's only natural, after all, for people to have a soft
spot for their own conceits, just as the crow and the monkey
dote on their young.

'Now in this gathering of people who are either envious of
others or dazzled by themselves, should someone raise a matter
that he has either read about as done in other times or witnessed in other places, those present behave as though their
whole reputation for wisdom were jeopardized, and as if they
would henceforward be rated as fools unless they were able to
expose faults in the proposal. If other strategies fail they fall
back on some such remark as, "The way we do it was good
enough for our forebears; if only we could match them in
wisdom!" Having uttered this as though it were a resounding
conclusion to the matter, they take their seats, implying that it
would be highly dangerous if anyone were found to be wiser in
some respect than his ancestors. In reality, we dismiss the best
ideas that they pass down to us without a qualm, but when
there's some point where they could have shown more sense we
immediately seize on that precedent with enthusiasm and cling
to it come what may. Such proud, ridiculous and stubborn
judgements I have come across in many places, once even in
England.'

'What's this?' I asked. 'Were you really in my country?'

'I was there for several months,' he replied, 'not long after
the rebellion of the west-countrymen against the King had been
crushed with their pitiable slaughter.[11] During my stay I was
much indebted to the most reverend father John Morton, Archbishop of Canterbury, and at that time also Chancellor of
England.[12] He, my dear Peter, was a man (More already knows
what I'm going to say), who was no less respected for his
wisdom and integrity than for his office. He was of average
height, and yielded nothing to age despite his advancing years.
His face inspired respect rather than fear. In conversation his
manner was easy, but at the same time serious and focused. He
liked to test those who came to him with petitions by speaking
to them sharply, though never offensively, in order to gauge

their spirit and presence of mind; provided that they kept within the bounds of respect, he was delighted to encounter qualities of character similar to his own, and he valued these as appropriate for anyone engaged in active affairs. In speech he was elegant and to the point. His mastery of the law was comprehensive, and he combined exceptional intelligence with a prodigious memory, having enhanced these natural talents by study and practice. The King relied heavily on his guidance and, while I was there, he appeared to be the guiding force behind much public policy. While still virtually a boy he had been whisked from school to court, and all his life he had been immersed in important matters, constantly tossed about by the shifts of fortune, so that in the midst of many great dangers he had learned a practical wisdom which, when it's acquired in this way, isn't easily forgotten.

'It happened one day when I was dining at his table that there was a certain layman present, one skilled in the laws of your country.[13] For some obscure reason he began to praise the rigorous justice that was then being dealt out to thieves: you could see them everywhere, he said, as many as twenty strung up on the same gallows. And yet, he declared, he was baffled that so many thieves, like some plague, remained a threat everywhere, when so few of them escaped punishment. Since I felt able to speak freely in front of the Cardinal, I replied, "That's nothing to be surprised about. For this manner of punishing thieves goes beyond justice, and brings no public benefit: as a penalty for theft it's too severe, but as a deterrent it's inadequate. Simple theft isn't so great a crime that it merits death, and yet no other punishment is severe enough to keep from robbery those who have no alternative means of supporting themselves. In this respect you, along with a good part of the world, appear to imitate bad schoolmasters who prefer beating their pupils to teaching them. Harsh and blood-chilling punishments are imposed for theft when it would make a lot more sense to ensure that people have the means to live, so that no one would face the dreadful necessity first of stealing and then of dying for it."

'"Adequate provision has been made for that already," replied the lawyer. "There are manual crafts and there's farming;

men can support themselves by these, unless they freely choose crime."

'"You're not going to wriggle out of it that way," I said. "For a start we can leave out those who so often return home from foreign or domestic wars crippled, as recently from the Cornish conflict and not long before that from the French wars.[14] These men sacrifice their limbs for the community or for the King, and their disability prevents them from practising their old trades, while they are too old to learn new ones. But, as I say, let's leave them out of consideration, because wars are irregular occurrences; let's focus on what happens every day. There's a great number of noblemen who, just like drones,[15] live idly off the labours of others, such as the tenants of their estates whom they cut to the bone with soaring rents (that is the only thriftiness they know, being in all else extravagant to the verge of bankruptcy). They drag along with them a great mob of useless retainers who have never acquired any skill by which they could make a living. These, as soon as their master dies or they fall sick themselves, are promptly thrown out, for it's preferable to support idlers rather than invalids, and often the dead man's heir is initially unable to maintain his father's establishment. Meanwhile those turned out promptly set about starving, unless they promptly set about thieving. What alternative do they have? At length, when a wandering life has taken the gloss off their clothing and off their health, when they are tainted by sickness and dressed in rags, no one of rank deigns to take them on and the peasants won't risk it. The latter don't need to be told that one who has been softly brought up in idleness and pleasure and been accustomed to staring out the neighbourhood with his sword, buckler and threatening gaze, disdaining all before him, will never be fit to work with a spade or hoe, nor will he faithfully serve a poor man for scant wages and a spare diet."

'"But," he fired back, "this is precisely the type of man we ought to encourage. Since they have a more aspiring and noble spirit than tradesmen or farmers, in time of war they provide the vigour and backbone of the army."

'"On that basis," I replied, "you might as well argue that thieves should be encouraged for the sake of wars, for as long as you have men like these you'll never be short of thieves. Thieves are no more reluctant to be soldiers than soldiers are reluctant to be thieves, so closely are the two callings related. But this problem, though it's familiar here, is by no means yours alone; it's common to nearly all nations. France, for instance, suffers from an even worse plague: the whole country is crowded, even in peacetime (if you can call it peace!), with mercenaries who are recruited on those very grounds that you propose for the maintenance of idle retainers here. It's the belief of wise-fools[16] that public safety is dependent on having a reliable and resolute defence force in readiness, ideally of veterans as they have no confidence in troops who are not battle-hardened. In consequence they seek pretexts for war out of fear they'll end up with inexperienced soldiers, and so men's throats are cut for nothing – just in case 'hand and spirit grow dull from lack of practice', as Sallust drily puts it.[17] Yet how dangerous it is to support such untamed beasts France has learned to her cost, and the examples of the Romans, the Carthaginians, the Syrians and many other nations tell the same story; for not only their sovereignty but their fields and cities have at one time or another been overthrown by standing armies. That these are less than necessary is shown by the example of the French military who, having been trained in arms from their infancy, nonetheless can't boast that they often return victorious from an encounter with your conscripts.[18] But I'll say no more on this in case I seem to be flattering the present company. It's a fact that, apart from those who are physically unfit for acts of strength or daring, or those whose spirit has been broken by domestic poverty, neither your urban tradesmen nor your rustic farm hands are supposed to be much in awe of those leisured parasites of the privileged. So there's no danger that strong and fit bodies (the only sort that the gentry deign to corrupt), which at the moment are either enfeebled by idleness or enervated by womanish occupations, would be at risk if they were taught the relevant skills to make a living and trained to manly labours. In any case, it seems to me that it in no way serves the public interest to maintain, against the eventuality of war, a whole crowd of people who disturb the peace. You never have war unless you wish for it, and there are always stronger grounds for peace than for war. But this is not the only cause that leads to theft; there is another one, in my view, which is peculiar to you English."

'"And what might that be?" asked the Cardinal.

'"Your sheep," I replied, "which are usually so meek and modest in their diet, have now, so it's claimed, begun to be so voracious and fierce that they swallow up people: they lay waste and depopulate fields, dwellings and towns. It's a fact that in those parts of the kingdom that produce the finest and thus most highly priced wool, the nobles, the gentry and even some abbots – godly men – are no longer content with the annual profits that their estates yielded to their predecessors. It's not enough for them that while living in idleness and luxury they contribute nothing to society, they must do it active harm. They leave nothing to the plough but enclose everything for pasture; they throw down homes and destroy communities, leaving just the church to function as a sheep fold.[19] And, as if there were not enough land in your country wasted already on chases and game reserves, these good men turn all habitations and arable fields into a wilderness. Consequently, just so that one insatiable glutton, a grim plague to his native land, can merge fields and enclose thousands of acres within a single boundary, the workers of the countryside are driven out. Some are stripped of their possessions, whether they are cheated by fraud or intimidated by force or, simply, worn down by wrongs and forced to sell them. So, one way or another, it turns out that these unhappy people have to leave – men, women, husbands, wives, orphans, widows, parents with small children, a company more numerous than rich since rural occupations require many hands – all these, as I say, have to leave their known and familiar homes without finding any place to take them in. They are evicted so briskly that all their household effects, which wouldn't fetch much even if they were able to wait for a buyer, are sold off for next to nothing. Since such a small sum is soon used up in the course of their wanderings, what alternative do they have but to steal and be hanged – according to the forms of law, naturally – or to continue their travels and beg? But in that case they are liable to be thrust into prison as vagrants since no one will employ them, although they are all too willing to work: since there are no crops to be sown there is no call for their particular skills. After all, just one shepherd or cowherd is perfectly adequate to graze livestock over an area that previously required many hands to make it yield its harvest.

'"This is the reason why food prices have soared in many places. In addition, the price of raw wool has risen so sharply that those poor people in your country who used to make it into cloth can't possibly afford to buy it, and as a result many are forced out of work into idleness. One cause of this is that after the hasty expansion of grazing land a wasting disease wiped out huge numbers of the sheep, rather as though God were punishing greed by inflicting on the beasts a plague that ought rightly to fall on the heads of their owners. And yet, even if the numbers of sheep should rise dramatically, the price won't fall; for although one can't speak about a monopoly as it isn't controlled by a single man, yet the wool trade is most certainly an oligopoly. It's in the hands of a small group of rich men who are under no necessity to sell before it suits them, and it only suits them when they can get their price. Then again, and for much the same reason, the price of other kinds of livestock is equally exorbitant and even more so since, what with the destruction of farms and the contraction of agriculture, there's no one left to oversee breeding. For these rich men won't rear calves as they do lambs but buy them lean and cheap from elsewhere, fatten them on their own pasture, and sell them on at an inflated price. So far as I can judge the full impact of this dubious arrangement has yet to be felt: up till now the dealers have only distorted prices in those areas where they sell, but since for some time they have been removing animals from other areas faster than they can be bred, a gradually diminishing supply at source must inevitably lead to acute shortages. In this way your island, which had seemed especially fortunate in this respect, will face disaster as the consequence of unbridled greed. For the soaring price of food is the reason why everyone is shedding as many members of his household as possible, and what can these do then but beg or, as men with a bit of spirit, turn to robbery?

'"What makes this poverty and abject need so much worse is that it exists alongside unbridled luxury. The servants of the nobility, along with trades-people and even peasants – in fact people of all social levels – are given to inappropriate display in their dress and lavish excess in food and drink.[20] Take eating houses, brothels, or those equally seedy places, wine-bars and tap-rooms; and then there are those dodgy games of chance like dice, cards, backgammon, tennis, bowling or quoits: don't all these swallow up the money of their adepts and send them off to steal? Root out these evil plagues. Insist that those who have ruined farms and villages either repair them or hand them over to others who are willing to recover and rebuild them. Let there be fewer kept in idleness. Let agriculture be restored and wool-working likewise, so that there may be proper jobs to occupy the horde of idlers, whether we are talking about those whom penury has already nudged into thieving or those who as yet are just vagrants or redundant servants but are sure to become thieves in the future.

'"It's perfectly obvious that, unless you cure these evils, it's futile to boast of the justice you display in punishing theft, since it's more specious than equitable or effective. If you permit the young to be viciously brought up and their characters steadily corrupted from early years, and then at length punish them for doing as adults what they have been destined for since childhood, what else is this but turning people into thieves and then punishing them for being such?"

'Even while I was saying these things, the lawyer prepared himself to respond, adopting that formal manner used by disputants who are better at recalling arguments than replying to them, so highly do they rate the art of memory. "You have spoken very well," he said, "especially for a visitor who has clearly heard a lot more about these matters than you have been able to find out first hand, as I will now demonstrate to you in a few words. Thus first of all, I will rehearse what you have said in due order, and then I will show how ignorance of our practices has misled you. Finally, I shall take your arguments apart and refute them. So, to begin with the first point, as I promised, it seems to me that there are four—"

'"That's enough," interrupted the Cardinal. "If you carry on like that, you're hardly likely to respond with a few words. Just for now we'll spare you the obligation of replying but reserve your right to do so for your next encounter, which I'd like to have tomorrow if that suits you and Raphael. But meanwhile I want to hear from you, my dear Raphael, why theft should not be punished with the ultimate penalty, or what other sentence you'd propose which might better serve the public interest. You can hardly consider that it should go unpunished; even as it is, with the prospect of death, people still rush headlong into stealing. What inhibition or fear would hold them back once they were sure of their lives, as you suggest? They would regard mitigation of the penalty as a reward, an invitation to offend."

'"It appears to me, kind and most reverend father," I replied, "that to take away someone's life for taking away money is wholly unjust. Indeed, I hold that nothing that's subject to fortune can be weighed against the value of a human life. If it's argued that this penalty requites the injury done to justice or the violation of the laws, rather than the actual money involved, then what else can this extreme justice fittingly be called but extreme injury?[21] We shouldn't approve laws so like Manlian orders[22] that the sword is unsheathed for the smallest violation, nor should we adopt the Stoic maxim that all crimes are equal.[23] By this they conclude that there is no distinction between killing a man and taking his money: but, if equity means anything, there is no similarity or relation between the two offences. God has forbidden us to kill anyone, and will we do it so readily for stealing some small change? If it should be argued that God's ban on taking life doesn't apply where human law admits the death penalty, then what's to prevent men from settling among themselves just how far rape, adultery and perjury ought to be tolerated? Bearing in mind that God has denied us the right to take not only the life of another but even our own, if the general consensus among nations over laws for killing each other carries sufficient force to exempt their agents from this ban and so permits them to kill – without any precedent from God – those condemned by human decrees, doesn't this subordinate that precept of divine law to human justice? The result will be that in the same way people will decide in everything just how far it suits them to follow God's laws. And, finally, the law of Moses was unyielding and severe, directed at a slavish and stubborn people, but it still punished theft with a fine rather than death.[24] We shouldn't suppose that God in his new law of mercy, like a father ruling his children, has given us greater licence to be cruel to one another.

'"These, then, are the reasons why I regard your punishment for theft as unjust. It must be obvious to anyone just how absurd it is to punish theft and murder in the same way. Once the thief realizes that theft carries no less a penalty than if he were convicted of murder, then that thought alone will drive him to kill the victim, whom otherwise he might just have robbed. Quite apart from the fact that he stands in no greater jeopardy if caught, there's greater safety in murder and a better hope of concealment if he gets rid of the witness. So, while we try to scare thieves with our severity, we are actually encouraging the killing of the innocent.

'"Now, as to that well-worn topic of what punishment may be more fitting: in my judgement it's a lot easier to find one that's an improvement than one that's worse. The Romans were highly experienced in the arts of government, so why do we doubt the efficacy of their penal code? With them, those convicted of especially heinous crimes were sent off in chains to work as slaves for life in stone quarries and mines. However, on this issue I can think of no system that has impressed me more than that which I encountered during my travels in Persia, among those commonly known as the Polylerites. This is a people who are neither small in numbers nor ill-governed, and apart from the annual tribute that they pay to the King of Persia, in all other matters they are independent and subject to their own laws. They are remote from the sea and almost wholly encircled by mountains, and since they are content with their own produce (the land being far from infertile) they have very little traffic with other countries. In accordance with their ancient customs, they have no interest in extending their frontiers and they are easily protected from any aggression by the mountains and by the pension that they pay to their over-lord. In consequence, they are spared military adventures and follow an existence that is comfortable rather than imposing, being more directed to happiness than nobility or renown. I suspect, in fact, that their name is scarcely known to any but their immediate neighbours.

'"It is their practice that those found guilty of theft repay whatever they have taken to the owner, and not to the prince as happens elsewhere. They consider that the ruler has just about as much right to the stolen goods as the thief himself. But if the property can't be retrieved, its equivalent value is taken from the thief's possessions and repaid and whatever remains over is given in full to his wife and children. The thief himself is con-demned to penal servitude.

'"Unless their crime was accompanied by violence, thieves are neither imprisoned nor shackled but are employed, free and unconstrained, in doing public works. Those who refuse to work or are half-hearted aren't put in chains, but they are urged on with the whip. For those who work hard there is no degrad-ing treatment, but at night after roll call they are locked in their cells. Except for the unremitting labour, their life isn't harsh: as workers for the public benefit they are decently fed at public expense, the arrangements varying from place to place. In some areas the costs are covered by alms, an arrangement that may sound unreliable but as the people themselves are so kind-hearted there is none more effective. Elsewhere the costs may be met from public funds, or else an individual tax is levied to provide support. In other areas again, the prisoners do no public work, but anyone in need of hired labour can go to the market place and secure the services of one for a fixed rate by the day. The cost is a bit less than that for a free man, and it is lawful to whip those who slack. So it works out that the prison-ers are never unemployed and each of them, in addition to covering his own costs, brings in a little daily income for the public treasury.

'"All the convicts, and they alone, are dressed in garments of a distinctive colour; their hair is not shaved but clipped a little

above the ears, and the tip of one ear is cut off. They are allowed
to receive food, drink and clothes of the approved colour from
their friends, but giving them money is a capital offence, both
for the donor and the recipient. It is equally dangerous for any
free man to take money from them, whatever the reason, or for
slaves (for so they call those convicted) to handle weapons.
Each of them wears a badge specific to their district, and it is a
capital offence to discard it, just as it is to be spotted outside
the confines of their own district or to speak with a slave from
another one. Plotting to escape is no less risky than the attempt
itself: in fact, to be an accomplice in such a plot entails death
for a slave and slavery for a free man. Set against that, rewards
are offered to informers: money for a free man and liberty for
a slave, and for both of them pardon and immunity from punishment for any complicity. As a result it can never be safer to
stick with a criminal project than to turn back from it.

'"These are the laws and practices relating to thieves, just as
I have described them, and it's easy to see how humane and
effective they are. The severity of the law is directed to destroy
vices and save men, so treating them that they can't help but be
good, devoting the remainder of their days to reparation as
once they gave themselves to crime. There is so little fear of a
relapse to their old conduct that travellers about to undertake
a journey consider slaves to be the most reliable guides, changing them at the boundary of each district. In fact, the slaves
have no scope for carrying out a robbery: they are unarmed,
and any money found on them would reveal their crime. If they
are caught punishment awaits them, and there is no hope of
escaping elsewhere. By what means can someone whose clothes
are quite unlike those in common use disguise himself and slip
away, unless he goes naked? And even then his clipped ear
would give him away. But is there not at least the danger that
the slaves may conspire together against the authorities? As if
the slaves of a single district stood a hope unless they sounded
out those in many other districts and won them over – and yet
that possibility is remote since they are forbidden to meet or
talk together, or even to greet each other. It seems scarcely cred-
ible that anyone could cheerfully confide such a plan to his

fellow slaves when they know well just how dangerous it is to keep the secret and how very profitable to betray it. More than that, no one is without the hope of winning freedom eventually, by being biddable and submissive, and giving good hope of amendment for the future. Not a year passes, in fact, in which some slaves aren't set free for patient acceptance of their punishment."

'After I had finished this account, I added that I could see no reason why this model might not be adopted in England, and with far better effect than that justice so highly rated by our legal expert. To which he, the common lawyer, replied, "A system like this could never be established in England without putting public order in the gravest danger." Having pronounced this he shook his head, pulled a long face and then fell silent, while all those present fell over themselves to endorse his opinion.

'At that point the Cardinal intervened: "It's not easy to guess whether such a scheme would turn out well or otherwise, since it has never been put to the test. Conceivably, when the death sentence had been pronounced on a criminal, the King might suspend its execution, at the same time banning any right to sanctuary,[25] and it could then be established whether the practice was viable. If the outcome was positive, it would be right to make it permanent; but if it turned out otherwise, the penalty of the law could still be inflicted on those already condemned. Either way, it would be no less in the public interest and no more unjust than if the sentence had been carried out at once. More than that, it seems clear to me that it would be no bad thing to treat vagrants in the same manner – for so far we've passed many laws against them but with precious little result."

'When the Cardinal had proposed this, all those who had sneered when I gave my version outdid each other in their enthusiasm; in particular, they liked the bit about vagrants, since it had been the Cardinal's own addition.

'I don't know whether it might not be as well to keep quiet about what followed, for it was a bit ridiculous, but I'll tell it nonetheless since there's no harm in it and it has some bearing on our subject. There was a certain parasite there who fancied himself in the role of a fool but played it in such a way that he seemed more like the real thing; his efforts at humour fell so flat that the man prompted more laughter than his jokes. But now and then something emerged that wasn't wholly absurd, so proving the adage that one who throws the dice often enough will eventually get a Venus.[26] One of the guests made the point that in my speech I had provided for thieves, just as the Cardinal had done for vagrants, so it only remained to take care of those forced into poverty and rendered incapable of supporting themselves by sickness or old age.

'"Leave it to me," said the fool, "for I'll see that it's properly arranged. These are just the kind of people I'm keen to get rid of: all too often they get on my nerves as they whinge and wail and demand money, though they never chirp persuasively enough to extract a single penny from me. In fact, it always turns out one of two ways: either it doesn't suit me to give, or it isn't possible anyway as there's nothing to give. Now it's beginning to dawn on them and when they see me coming they spare themselves the effort and let me pass in silence; heaven knows, they expect no more from me now than if I were a priest. For my part, I'd introduce a law that these beggars be divided up and packed off to Benedictine monasteries where the men could become lay-brothers, as they are called, and all the women I should compel to become nuns."

'The Cardinal smiled and passed it off as a joke, but all the rest took it literally. However, a certain friar, a theologian, was so delighted with this hit at the expense of priests and monks that he too joined in the game, although he was generally solemn to the point of gloom. "But you won't get rid of the beggars," he said, "unless you provide for us friars as well."[27]

'"That's been sorted already," replied the parasite, "since the Cardinal provided for you most elegantly when he proposed that vagrants should be rounded up and put to work, for you are the most notorious vagrants of all."

'At this the entire company, who were keeping a sharp eye on the Cardinal and saw that he didn't disapprove, joined in the mockery – with the exception of the friar. Unsurprisingly, he was stung by the vinegar[28] and flared up in such a rage that he couldn't hold back his abuse: he called the man an idle wretch, a slanderer, a stirrer of discord and a son of perdition,[29] invoking the most blood-chilling threats from sacred scripture. And now the jester began his work in earnest, since he was on his home ground.

'"Don't be angry, good brother," he said, "for it is written, *In your patience you shall possess your souls.*"[30]

'To this the friar retorted (and I'm using his very words), "I'm not angry, you hang-dog, or at least I don't sin, for the Psalmist says, *Be angry, and sin not.*"[31]

'At this the Cardinal gently cautioned the friar to calm himself, but he replied, "No, my lord, I speak only out of holy zeal, as I ought. For holy men have had holy zeal, which is why it is said, *The zeal of your house has eaten me up,*[32] and as we sing in the liturgy, *Those who mocked Elisha as he went up to the house of God, felt the zeal of the baldhead.*[33] So, too, may this mocker, this clown, this depraved wretch feel its force."

'"I dare say you mean well," said the Cardinal, "but you would seem to me to act, if not in a holier, at least in a wiser way, if you didn't match yourself against a blockhead and take on this foolish dispute with a foolish man."

'"No, my lord," he returned, "I would not act more wisely. For Solomon, that wisest of men, says, *Answer a fool according to his folly,*[34] just as I'm doing now. I'm showing him the pit into which he'll fall if he's not very careful. For if the many mockers of Elisha – who was just one bald man – felt the zeal of a baldhead, how much more will it be felt by a single mocker of many friars, among whom there are many baldheads.[35] And what's more, we have a papal bull by which all those who mock us are excommunicated."[36]

'The Cardinal, when he saw that there was no end in sight, sent the parasite packing with a nod and tactfully redirected the conversation. Shortly afterwards he rose from table to attend to those clients who had business to discuss, and dismissed us.

'Now just look, my dear More, at the lengthy account that I've inflicted on you. I would have been ashamed to spend so much time on it, if you hadn't insisted so eagerly and seemed to listen as if you didn't want anything left out. I ought really to have related it more briefly, but I felt obliged to give a full account in order to expose the mentality of those who turned a deaf ear to what I suggested, but then were in favour of it the moment they saw that the Cardinal didn't disapprove. They were so subservient to him that they applauded – and very nearly took seriously – the fantasies of a fool, which their master had tolerated as a joke. From this you can see just how courtiers would regard me or my counsels.'

'Indeed, my dear Raphael,' I replied, 'you have given me great pleasure, for all that you've said has been wise and witty. But more than that, as you spoke I seemed not only to be back in my native land but somehow to be a boy again, and all through that happy reminiscence of the Cardinal in whose household I grew up. You were already valued by me in other respects, Raphael, but you can hardly imagine how much dearer you are now because you are so devoted to his memory. All the same, nothing alters my opinion: it seems obvious to me that if only you could overcome your horror of princes' courts your counsel would be an important asset to public welfare. As a good man, you have no greater obligation than this. Your friend Plato holds that commonwealths will only be happy when either philosophers rule or rulers philosophize:[37] how remote happiness must appear when philosophers won't even deign to share their thoughts with kings.'

'They're not so self-centred,' replied Raphael, 'that they wouldn't happily share their thoughts; indeed, many have already done so in published books, if only those in power were prepared to take their good advice. But it's evident that Plato was right to suppose that unless kings became philosophers themselves they would never accept the counsels of philosophers, seeing that they are warped and corrupted by false values from childhood. This is what he experienced for himself in the case of Dionysius.[38] If I proposed sound laws to some king and tried to eradicate the sources of evil within him, don't you think that I would be summarily thrown out or made an object of ridicule?

'Now imagine,[39] just for a moment, that I am at the court of
the King of France and seated in his council: the King is personally presiding over a circle of his most experienced advisers, in
secret session, as they work out by what cunning devices he can
keep Milan under his control and win back the elusive prize of
Naples, after which he can go on to overthrow the Venetians
and so dominate all Italy; next, how he may bring Flanders,
Brabant and eventually the whole of Burgundy under his rule,
along with several other nations that he has long been minded
to invade.[40] One councillor urges him to make an alliance with
the Venetians, designed to last just as long as it suits his own
interests, adopting a common strategy with them and even
allowing them a share of the spoils, since that can always be
clawed back once the goal has been achieved; another councillor, meanwhile, advises hiring German mercenaries, another
suggests keeping the Swiss neutral with cash, and someone else
proposes appeasing the ruffled sanctity of the Emperor with
some sacred offering, like gold; yet another deems it a priority
to reach a settlement with the King of Aragon and considers
that, as a guarantee of peace, he should be given someone else's
kingdom of Navarre; at the same time it is suggested that the
Prince of Castile should be ensnared with the prospect of a
marriage alliance, and that a number of the nobles at his court
should be brought onside by regular pensions. The most intrac-
table problem to present itself is: what in the meanwhile to do
about England? It's agreed that peace should be discussed and
that the alliance, always unreliable, ought to be reinforced with
strong links: let the English be called allies, and yet suspected as
enemies; let the Scots be stood like sentinels at their post, poised
to strike at once should the English make any move; and then
a banished nobleman with claims to the English throne must be
encouraged secretly (seeing that treaties forbid doing it openly)
in order to provide some hold over a prince that they don't
trust.[41] Now, in the middle of such weighty deliberations, with
so many distinguished men outdoing each other with proposals
for war, how would it be if a nobody like me were to stand up
and propose a totally different tack – that in my view Italy
should be left alone and the King should stay at home; that the

kingdom of France on its own is already too much for one man
to govern effectively, and the King shouldn't dream of adding
on any more; and suppose that then I put before them the
legislation of the Achorians, a people who are to be found to
the south-east of the Isle of the Utopians? Once upon a time
they had gone to war so that their king could gain possession
of another kingdom, which he claimed as his hereditary right
through some ancient marriage pact; once they had achieved
this aim, they saw that holding on to it was likely to prove no
less trouble than acquiring it had been; the seeds of trouble
were forever sprouting among their new subjects, both through
internal revolt and incursions from outside, and so they were
permanently at war, whether on behalf of these new subjects or
against them, with no prospect of standing down their own
army. In the meantime, moreover, they were being fleeced:
money was pouring out of the country, their blood was being
spilt for someone else's vanity, and peace was nowhere in sight;
at home sedition was widespread, so that thieving became
second nature, and life was held cheap; law fell into contempt
because the king was caught up with the cares of two kingdoms
and couldn't give due attention to either. When they saw that
there was no end to this catalogue of evils, the Achorians delib-
erated together and very politely offered their king the option
of retaining whichever of the two kingdoms he preferred, for he
couldn't govern them both. They declared themselves to be far
too numerous to be ruled by half a king, just as no one willingly
takes on a mule driver that he's got to share with someone else.
The worthy prince was then compelled to be content with his
original kingdom and to pass the new one on to a friend, who
was ejected from it soon afterwards.

'Further, suppose I showed that all this warmongering, by
which so many nations were reduced to chaos in the King of
France's interests, would finally, when it had emptied his treasury and worn down the people, come to nothing through some
quirk of fortune. He ought therefore to care for the kingdom
inherited from his ancestors, adorn it and nurture its fullest
potential;[42] he should love his people and be loved by them, live
among them and govern them gently; and, as to other king-

doms, he should leave them well alone, since that which had already fallen to his lot was enough, and more than enough. Now tell me, my dear More, how do you think such a speech would be received?'

'None too favourably,' I replied.

'Well,' he said, 'let's continue. Suppose that the councillors of some king[43] are deliberating with him and working out schemes by which they can amass more treasure for him: one of them urges him to raise the value of money whenever he has to pay out, and to depress it below the proper rate whenever it's his turn to collect – in this way he can pay off a large debt with less money, and recover a lot on a small one; another suggests that he should pretend to go to war and raise money on that pretext, then, at the right moment, he can make peace with solemn and sacred ceremonies, by these means deluding the common people who will see him as a godly prince, reluctant to shed blood; yet another councillor puts him in mind of certain ancient and musty laws, long out of use, which (since no one remembers them being made) everyone has broken, and proposes that the king imposes fines for violating them – there's no more fruitful or honourable source of income than one bearing the mask of justice; meanwhile it's suggested that by means of heavy fines he places numerous activities under a ban, especially those against the public good, and later, for cash, he can grant dispensations to those whose interests are affected by the ban; in this way he gains popular esteem and yet makes a double profit, from the fines levied on those whose cupidity has drawn them into his trap, and from the exemptions he sells to others; here, indeed, the higher the price the better the prince, seeing that he is reluctant to grant any private person concessions that clash with the public good, and consequently will only do so at a great price. One individual urges him to put pressure on the judges so that they will settle every case in the crown's favour and, in addition, advises that they be summoned to the palace and invited to discuss the king's affairs in his presence; in this way there'll be no cause of his, however patently unjust, in which one of the judges, whether from a desire to contradict or a determination to be different, or just in order to curry favour, won't hit upon some loophole by which trickery can be introduced; so through the conflicting views of the judges even a clear-cut issue becomes controversial and truth itself is brought in question, while the prince is given scope to interpret the law in his own interest; the rest of the judges will fall into line, either from the urge to conform or from fear, and after this the Bench can hand down judgement without a qualm. There is never any shortage of pretexts for ruling on the prince's behalf: it is good enough for him whether equity is on his side, or the letter of the law, or the distorted reading of some document, or that which – in the last resort – outweighs all laws for the conscientious judge, the indisputable prerogative of the prince.

'Then all the councillors endorse the maxim of Crassus,[44] that a prince who maintains an army can never have enough treasure; and on top of that, that he can do no wrong,[45] however much he may want to, for all property belongs to him, as do the persons of his subjects: each one of them owns only as much as the prince, in his generosity, chooses not to take away; it's in the prince's interest to keep this to a minimum, seeing that his own security depends on preventing the people from getting too familiar with riches and freedom, since these make them reluctant to put up with harsh and unjust commands – need and poverty, by contrast, break their spirits, render them submissive, and take from the oppressed the aspiring spirit of rebellion.[46]

'Now what if, at this point, I were to get up once again and assert that all these proposals are both shameful and dangerous to the king, whose honour and even safety depend on the wealth of the people rather than on his own? Suppose I showed that the people choose a king for their own sake, not for his, so that thanks to his efforts and exertions they may live in comfort and security; that it is the duty of the prince to put the well-being of his people before his own, in the very way that it is the function of any shepherd worthy of the name to feed his sheep rather than himself. Experience shows just how wrong those are who think that the poverty of the people is a guarantee of peace – where will you find more brawling than among beggars? Who's keener to turn things upside-down than the person who is most dissatisfied with his present manner of life? And then, who's more reckless about attacking the established order in hope of gain than the man with nothing to lose? If a king is so despised and detested by his subjects that he can't keep them in order unless he browbeats them with threats, extortion and confiscation, reducing them to beggary, then it would be better for him to abdicate than retain his throne by such means that even though he may retain the title he loses all the majesty of a king – ruling over beggars doesn't befit the dignity of a king; he must have contented and prosperous subjects. This is certainly what was meant by Fabricius,[47] that upright and high-minded man, when he stated that he would rather rule over the rich than be rich himself; and certainly, for some single person to indulge in pleasure and delights while surrounded by the weeping and lamentation of others is not to be the governor of a kingdom but of a gaol; finally, just as it's a pretty useless doctor who only knows how to cure a disease by inflicting another one, so he who knows no other way to improve the lives of citizens except by taking away the amenities of life is admitting that he doesn't know how govern free men. Instead he ought to curb either his sloth or his pride, since these are the vices that most frequently lead the people to despise or hate him; let him live harmlessly on his own resources and match his expenses to his income; let him reduce crime, and keep his subjects from it by wise governance rather than allowing it to grow and then punishing it; let him be cautious about reviving laws that custom has annulled, especially those long out of use which have never been missed, and let him never seize anything, under the guise of a fine, that would render an ordinary citizen unjust and deceitful in the eyes of the law for claiming it.

'Now suppose that here I put before them the law of the Macarians, a people situated not so far from the Utopians, whose king on the day that inaugurates his reign takes an oath reinforced by solemn rites never to have in his treasury at any one time more than a thousand pounds in gold, or the equivalent in silver. This law, they maintain, was established by an admirable king, one more concerned for the good of his country than for his personal wealth, in order to block the accumula-

tion of so much money that it impoverished the people. He
reckoned that this sum would be adequate for a king to oppose
rebels or the kingdom to resist invaders, but would not be
enough to encourage any ideas about invading others, and this
was the main purpose of the law. But another motive was to
ensure a ready supply of money for the daily business transac-
tions of the citizens, and since the crown was bound to pay out
whatever excess had accumulated in the treasury he judged
that no king would seek out opportunities for extortion. Such
a king will be dreaded by the corrupt and loved by all good
citizens. If, then, I were to force these ideas and others like them
on people fiercely committed to the opposite point of view,
would I not be preaching to the deaf?'

'Stone deaf,' I replied, 'without a shadow of doubt, and I can
hardly say that I'd be surprised. To speak frankly, it seems to
me pointless to urge propositions of this sort, or to proffer such
advice as you know will never be accepted. What good can it
do? How can such an alien line of argument touch those whose
minds are wholly taken over and possessed by the contrary
opinion? In a discussion among friends this sort of academic
philosophy is not without its charm, but in the councils of
princes, where major issues are debated with great authority,
it's quite out of place.'

'Exactly my point,' replied Raphael. 'Philosophy has no place
among princes.'

'That's certainly true,' I said. 'There is no place for that academic mode[48] which holds that you can discuss anything you
like, regardless of the setting. But there is another philosophy,
more attuned to public affairs, which knows its stage and
adapts itself to the play in hand, acting out its role fittingly and
with due decorum. This is the sort of philosophy you must use.
Otherwise it's as if, in the course of a play by Plautus when the
domestics are swopping jokes, you stride on stage in the guise
of a philosopher and declaim that speech in the *Octavia* where
Seneca disputes with Nero.[49] Wouldn't it be better to act a
dumb part than turn the whole thing into a tragi-comedy by
uttering such inappropriate lines? When you mix in alien ele-
ments, even if they are superior, you wreck the play; do the best

you can in the play that's actually in hand, and don't upset it because you happen to have thought of one that might be more entertaining.

'That's exactly how things are in public affairs and in the councils of princes. Even if you can't eradicate harmful ideas or remedy established evils, that's no reason to turn your back on the body politic: you mustn't abandon ship simply because you can't direct the winds. Equally, you shouldn't force strange and startling ideas on those with whom you know they'll carry no weight because their convictions run the other way. Instead, you must do your best to operate through an indirect approach, and try to handle everything tactfully, so that whatever you cannot turn to good will at least do the minimum of harm. After all, it's inconceivable that everything should turn out well unless all men become good, and that I don't anticipate for quite some time to come.'

'The only outcome of that approach,' he retorted, 'will be that while I try to remedy the insanity of others I shall end up raving with them. If I want to speak the truth then I'll have to do it my way. Whether it's the role of a philosopher to utter lies[50] I have no idea, but it's certainly not mine. My manner of speaking may well strike courtiers as tasteless and even offensive, but I don't see why it should seem odd to the point of absurdity. What if I were to tell them about the scheme that Plato imagines in his republic, or that which the Utopians actually practise in theirs? However superior these may be (and without question they are), all the same they would seem outlandish here because the rule is private ownership of property while there all things are held in common.

'Apart from the fact that those who have decided to stampede headlong down a different path are never pleased with the person who calls them back and points out its dangers, what was there in my speech that it mightn't be fitting – and even necessary – to say, whatever the context? If all those things that the warped standards of mankind have rendered odd are to be dismissed, then we Christians will have to jettison the bulk of Christ's teachings; yet he forbade us to ignore them – in fact, he ordered his disciples to proclaim from the rooftops what he had whispered in their ears.[51] The greater part of his teachings is more remote from the actual behaviour of mankind than was that speech of mine; and yet, when people have been reluctant to match their morals to the standard of Christ, canny preachers (no doubt following your advice) have accommodated his precepts to fit their morals, just like some leaden yardstick,[52] so that at least there might be some connection between the two. I can't see what this achieves except that people may be bad with a lighter conscience.

'And indeed this is just as much as I would achieve in the councils of princes. For I would think either differently from the others, which would be like having no thoughts at all, or the same, and be, as Mitio says in Terence, a colluder in their madness.[53] I just don't see what's behind that indirect approach of yours, by which you argue that every effort should be made to handle tactfully those matters which can't turn out well, so that they end up doing as little harm as possible. In such a setting there's no room for pretence or for looking the other way: you must openly support the worst counsels and endorse the vilest of policies. Anyone who gave lukewarm praise to evil advice would be rated a spy, even a traitor. Besides, there'll be no opportunities for you to do good once you are involved with colleagues who would more easily corrupt the best of men than be reformed themselves; either you will be corrupted by their evil customs or, if you hold on to integrity and innocence, you will be used as a screen for the dishonesty and folly of others, so far is that indirect approach from changing anything for the better.

'It is for this reason that Plato in a witty comparison states why wise men rightly steer clear of public affairs: they see people crowding onto the streets and getting soaked with incessant rain and they can't persuade them to go under a roof and get out of the wet. They know they will achieve nothing if they go out themselves apart from getting soaked as well, so they remain indoors and are content to keep themselves dry since they can't cure the folly of others.[54]

'Actually, my dear More, to be entirely frank it seems to me that wherever you have private property and all things are measured in terms of money it's all but impossible for a community to be just or prosperous, unless you consider that justice can function where the best things belong to the worst people, or that there can be happiness where everything is divided up among very few – and even those few derive little benefit while the remainder are thoroughly wretched.

'So, for that reason, when I reflect on the remarkably wise and holy institutions of the Utopians, who manage with a minimum of laws to run things so well that while virtue is rewarded yet there is abundance for all since everything is divided equally, I contrast their customs with those of so many other nations that are forever generating new laws but aren't satisfactorily regulated. In such nations whatever a man can obtain he calls his private property, but an almost constant stream of legislation is still not enough to ensure that he can secure it, or defend it, or even distinguish it from what another in his turn calls his private property, as is clearly shown by the infinite number of interminable law suits which are forever springing up. When, as I say, I reflect on these things, I'm drawn to Plato's view and feel less surprised that he declined to legislate for those people who rejected laws by which goods might be shared equally by all.[55] In fact, this wisest of men clearly saw that the one and only way to social well-being is equality of possessions; and I doubt whether this can ever be practised where each individual has his own property. For when everyone is entitled to claw together as much as he can get for himself, then, no matter how great the resources available, a small number end up dividing the whole lot among themselves, and the remainder are stuck in poverty. The usual outcome is that each group merits the fate of the other, since the former are grabbing, dishonest and unproductive and the latter are, by contrast, unpretentious and decent people whose daily labour brings more profit to the community than to themselves.

'So I am absolutely convinced that there can be no equitable or just distribution of goods, nor can the affairs of this world be conducted happily, unless private ownership is completely suppressed. But if it remains, by far the largest and best part of the human race will always be weighed down by an inevitable burden of poverty and insecurity. I admit that this burden can be alleviated to some small degree, but I maintain that it cannot be entirely removed. Doubtless, laws might be passed that no one should own more than a specified amount of land or that there be limits to the amount of money anyone can hold; again, others could be devised to prevent the prince from overreaching his powers and the populace from being insubordinate, or to ban the soliciting and sale of public offices and to restrict such expenses as these incur – for otherwise they provide a temptation to recoup costs through fraud or extortion and necessitate the preferment of rich men to offices more fittingly held by the wise. Laws of this kind might, I'd suggest, reduce and mitigate these evils in much the same way as a regular application of poultices can relieve the bodies of the incurably sick, but there is absolutely no hope of curing them and restoring good order as long as property remains private. Rather, as you strive to cure one part, you aggravate the sickness in others: so, by mutual exchange, the healing of one causes the disease in another, since you can't give something to one person without taking it away from someone else.'

'That's not how I see it,' I said. 'It's just not possible to live properly where all things are held in common. How can there be an adequate supply of goods if any individual can withdraw from work, seeing that he's not motivated by gain and is rendered lazy by reliance on the efforts of others? And then, when people are driven by necessity and yet no one has any legal claim to whatever he's gathered together, what can come of it but unceasing violence and disorder? All the more so when the authority and reverence due to magistrates have been jettisoned, for I can't see how they might be maintained among those who recognize no distinctions.'[56]

'It doesn't surprise me that it seems that way to you,' he replied, 'since you have no conception of such a polity, or at least a distorted one. You really should have been with me in Utopia and seen their manners and customs for yourself, just as I did; for I remained there for over five years, and would gladly never have left except to reveal that new world to others. If you had seen them, then you would freely admit that you had never seen a people anywhere so well regulated as they are.'

'All the same,' said Peter, 'you are going to have some difficulty persuading me that one can encounter in that new world a people better organized than in the world we know: our intelligence is no less than theirs and our governments, I imagine, are more ancient, so that long practice has introduced many things that enhance life, quite apart from those things hit upon by chance that unaided intelligence could never have devised.'

'As to the relative antiquity of governments,' responded Raphael, 'you'd be in a better position to judge if you had read the histories of their world: if these are to be trusted, they had cities there before there were inhabitants here. As to those things that either ingenuity has discovered or chance thrown up, they could have happened in either place. Besides, it is my firm belief that though we may outclass them by innate intelligence, they leave us behind when it comes to effort and the desire to learn. As their chronicles reveal, prior to our landing they had heard nothing about us Ultra-equatorials (for that's what they call us), except that some twelve hundred years previously a ship was wrecked on their island, having been driven there by a storm. A number of Romans and Egyptians were cast ashore and never left the place. Now just look how the Utopians through their diligence turned this single opportunity to their advantage: there was no useful skill within the entire Roman Empire that they didn't either learn under the guidance of their visitors or work out for themselves from hints they picked up. Such was the advantage they gained from this single occurrence, when some of our people were driven on their shore. If ever in the past a similar quirk of fate has brought someone from there over here, the event has been completely forgotten, just as in times to come, conceivably, it will be forgotten that I ever went there. From just one encounter they at once made their own whatever we had developed for the improvement of life, but I suspect that it will be a long time before we adopt any practice that they do better than us. As I see it, this is the basic reason why their affairs are more wisely ordered and they lead happier lives, although we are not inferior to them in aptitude or resources.'

'In that case, my dear Raphael,' I said, 'I beg and entreat you, do please describe that island to us. Don't try to keep it brief, but describe in sequence their fields, rivers, towns, inhabitants, manners, institutions, laws, and generally whatever you think we would want to know – and you can take it that we want to know everything that we don't know already.'

'There's nothing I would rather do,' he answered, 'for I have all these things vividly in my mind. But it will take up quite a lot of time.'

'Well, let's go in to lunch,' I said. 'Afterwards we can take all the time we need.'

'Agreed,' he replied. So we went in to lunch. After we had eaten we returned and settled on the same bench, and I ordered the servants to see that we weren't disturbed. Then Peter Giles and I urged Raphael to carry out his promise. So, when he saw us attentive and keen to hear him, he sat briefly in silent thought and then began as follows.

BOOK TWO

At the central point where it is widest the island of the Utopians extends out for two hundred miles, and nowhere does it get much narrower except where it tapers at the two ends. These ends, as if they enclosed a circle five hundred miles in circumference, give to the island the appearance of a crescent moon, the horns of which are some eleven miles apart. The sea flows between these into a huge bay protected from the winds by the encircling land, which is mostly not rough but calm, like a huge lake. Consequently almost the entire inner part of the island serves as a harbour, ships crossing it in all directions, to the general advantage of the natives.

What with shallows on the one hand and reefs on the other, the straits into the bay are perilous in the extreme. A single rock, which rises clear of the sea near the centre of the channel and is thus less of a danger, has a tower constructed on it that is manned by a garrison. The other rocks lie under the surface and are treacherous: the channels are known only to the islanders themselves, so it is highly unusual for foreigners to enter the bay unless they have a Utopian pilot. Indeed, the entrance is scarcely safe even for them unless they plot their course by markers fixed on the shore. Should these be shifted to different sites, they could easily lure the largest enemy fleet to destruction.

On the other side of the island there are frequent harbours, but all points of access are so fortified by nature or by contrivance that a mere handful of defenders can repel a powerful attacking force. A tradition – which is borne out by the lie of the land – claims that the country was not always surrounded by sea. Instead Utopus, who gave his name to the island by conquest (previously it had been known as Abraxa) and who raised its brutish and uncultivated inhabitants to such a level of civilization and humanity that they now outshine virtually all other nations, having gained victory at his very first landing, caused a channel fifteen miles wide to be excavated at that end of the peninsula joined to the mainland, so surrounding it with the sea. He put not only the natives to work on this project but his own troops as well, so that none would think the labour a disgrace. Since it was divided among so many, the task was completed with amazing speed, so that the neighbouring peoples, who initially mocked the folly of such a scheme, were struck with admiration and awe at its success.

The island has fifty-four cities, all spacious and imposing, which share the same language, customs, institutions and laws; the similarity extends to their layout, and as far as the site allows, to their appearance.[1] Those closest to each other are twenty-four miles apart, and none is so remote that it is more than a day's walk from another. Every year each city sends three mature and experienced citizens to Amaurot to deliberate on the affairs of the island. That particular city, placed as it were at the navel of the country and thus easily accessible to delegates from all parts, serves as the capital.

Agricultural land is so skilfully divided up between the cities that on no side does it extend for less than twelve miles, and on those sides where the towns are further apart it may be much more. No city wants to extend its boundaries since the people regard themselves as cultivators of the soil rather than its exploiters. At convenient intervals throughout the countryside they locate houses stocked with farming equipment, and these are occupied by town dwellers who take it in turns to live in the country. No rural household has fewer than forty members, men and women, as well as two slaves who are permanently attached to it. Each household is run by a responsible and mature couple, and over every thirty households is set a phylarch. Every year twenty persons from each household who have completed a two-year spell in the country return to the town and an identical number is sent out to take their place. These new arrivals are instructed by those who have already

been there for a year and are consequently more adept at farming and they, in their turn, will teach those who will arrive in
the following year. If all were equally raw and uninstructed in
agriculture they might adversely affect the food supply by their
lack of skill. This practice of alternating farm workers is the
established custom so that no one is forced to spend too long in
an arduous way of life against their will, yet many who take an
instinctive pleasure in work on the land are allowed to remain
for a number of years.

The farm workers till the soil, feed the animals, collect wood
and convey it to the city by the easiest route, whether by land
or water. They raise countless numbers of chicks by a remarkable method: rather than hens sitting on the eggs, they incubate
a great number of them at a warm, steady temperature and so
hatch them; the chicks, as soon as they emerge from the shells,
fix on the humans and follow them rather than their mothers.

They raise only a few horses, and those high-spirited, which
they keep solely to train younger men in the art of horseman-
ship. For all the work of cultivation and haulage they use
oxen, which they allow are inferior to horses where speed is
concerned but surpass them in endurance, and are, as they see
it, less prone to disease. They are also less trouble and expense
to keep, and once they are too old to work they can be used
for meat.

Grain they use only for bread, for they drink wine, cider or
perry, or plain water, and the latter frequently boiled with
honey or liquorice, of which they have ample supplies. Although
they measure with great accuracy just how much food each city
and its adjacent area consume, they nevertheless produce far
more grain and cattle than is necessary for their own use and
share the surplus with their neighbours. Whatever items of
equipment the farm dwellers need that can't be found in the
country they apply for to the city, and since no exchange is
involved they obtain their requirements from the city magistrates without any hassle. In any case, many of them go to the
city each month to observe the festival. When the time of harvest draws near the rural phylarchs inform the city magistrates
how many helpers will be needed. The harvesters arrive as a

body at the agreed time, and with favourable weather they can gather the entire crop within one day.

Their Cities, in particular Amaurot

Anyone who knows one of their cities knows the lot, for they are all as alike as the nature of the site allows. Accordingly I shall give a picture of just one of them, and it does not greatly matter which. But why not Amaurot? It is the pre-eminent city since the others defer to it as the seat of the federal senate; what's more, it is the best known to me as I lived there continuously for five years.

Now, Amaurot is seated against a gently sloping hill and is almost square in its layout. The shorter side begins just below the crest of the hill and runs down to the river Anyder; the side that then extends along the bank is rather longer. The Anyder rises in a small spring eighty miles above Amaurot, but other streams flow into it, two of them quite large, so that by the time it passes the city it is half a mile across. It continues, growing even larger, until after sixty miles it merges with the sea. The river is tidal for the whole stretch between the coast and the city and even some miles above, ebbing and flowing with a powerful current every six hours. As the sea comes in, its waves fill the course of the Anyder for thirty miles, pushing back the flow of the river; even further up it turns the water brackish, but beyond that the river sweetens and is fresh when it flows past the city.[2] As the tide ebbs, the wholesome water follows it almost to the mouth of the river.

The city is linked to the opposite bank of the river by a bridge that rests not on wooden supports or piles but on handsome stone-built spans. This stands at the upper end of the city, that which is furthest from the sea, so that ships can pass along its whole length without hindrance.[3] There is in addition a second stream, not so large but pleasant and tranquil, which rises in the hill on which the city stands and flows through its centre, following the slope of the land, before joining the waters of the Anyder. The source and head of this stream are just outside

the city, but the Amaurotans have included them within the
defensive walls in case, given a hostile attack, the enemy might
attempt to block and divert the waters or pollute them. Water
is distributed from this source to the lower parts of the city by
means of earthenware ducts, and where the character of the
ground prevents this, rain water collected in huge cisterns
proves just as effective.

The town is defended by a high, thick wall with numerous
towers and bastions, and on three sides this is enclosed by a dry
moat, deep as well as wide, and blocked with thorn hedges,
while on the fourth side the river itself acts as the moat. The
streets are laid out with a view both to the flow of traffic and to
protection from the wind. The buildings are far from mean,
with matching terraces facing each other along the length of
the street, the façades separated by a carriageway twenty feet
across. At the back of the houses is a large garden which extends
the length of the block and is wholly enclosed by the rear walls
of the buildings. No house is without doors opening both onto
the street and into the garden; these double doors, which yield
to a touch of the hand and close of themselves, permit anyone
to enter.[4] As a result no place is ever private: indeed they
exchange the actual houses by lot every tenth year.

The Utopians are devoted to their gardens and in them they
cultivate vines, fruit trees, herbs and flowers with such care and
skill that I have never seen any more productive or pleasing to
the eye. This enthusiasm for gardening derives not only from the
pleasure it gives of itself but also from the competition between
blocks for the best kept garden. Certainly, you won't easily
encounter anything in the entire city that is more useful and
delightful to the citizens, and for that reason it seems that the
founder of the city must have given priority to the creation of
such gardens. It is said that the basic plan of the city was laid
down at the outset by Utopus himself, but he left to posterity the
work of adornment and improvement, which he recognized
could hardly be achieved in a single lifetime. On the basis of
their records, which cover 1,760 years from the capture of the
island,[5] and are accurately and diligently preserved in writing,
the earliest houses were low, like huts or poor rustic dwellings,

and made from odd bits of timber, the walls rendered with mud and the conical roofs thatched with straw. But nowadays every house is three storeys high and elegantly constructed: the wall-facings are built of flint, quarry-stone or burned bricks, the inner cavity being filled with rubble. The roofs are now flat and covered with a form of cement that costs next-to-nothing but can withstand the threat of fire and is more weather resistant than lead. Draughts are excluded from the windows by means of glass (of which they have ample quantities), or sometimes by linen treated with clear oil or gum – which has the effect of making it both more translucent and more resistant to the wind.

Magistrates

Annually each group of thirty families elects an official, known in their ancient language as a syphogrant but now called a phylarch. Over every group of ten syphogrants is placed an officer originally called a tranibor and now a proto- or chief phylarch. In due course all the syphogrants, two hundred of them,[6] having sworn an oath to choose the man they judge best fitted, elect as governor by a secret ballot one out of four candidates put forward by the people, for one is chosen from each quarter of the city to be proposed to the senate. The governor's office is held for life, unless he is deprived on suspicion of favouring tyranny, while the tranibors face re-election every year, though they are not usually changed without good reason. The remaining officials hold office for a single year.

The tranibors attend on the governor in council every third day, and more often should business require it: there they discuss public affairs and resolve private disputes – that's if there should be any, for they are extremely rare. Two of the syphogrants are always admitted to meetings of the senate, a different pair each day. It is stipulated that no issue relating to the public interest may be settled unless it has been debated in the senate on three separate days, and it is a capital offence to devise schemes about public matters outside the senate or the popular assembly. The purpose behind these rules, they claim, is to prevent any conspiracy by the governor and the tranibors to alter the constitution and oppress the people. For this reason all issues judged to be of importance are referred to the assembly of syphogrants and they, having discussed the matter with the households they represent, consult among themselves and then report their conclusions to the senate. On occasion a question may be placed before the general council of the whole island. It's also accepted practice in the senate that business is never discussed on the day that it is raised, but deferred to the following session.[7] This is in case someone, after blurting out the first idea that enters his head, should then concentrate on bolstering his own proposals rather than those that might benefit the commonwealth, preferring to risk the general welfare rather than his own reputation, and all because of a perverse and stupid fear that he might have appeared too hasty at the outset. He should have had the sense in the first place to speak with due consideration rather than impetuosity.

Occupations

Agriculture is the one activity common to all, both men and women, and from which no one is exempt. They are instructed in it from childhood, partly in school where they learn the principles, and partly through expeditions to nearby farms where they learn as if through play,[8] not simply looking on but joining in the work as an opportunity for exercise. In addition to agriculture – which is, as I have said, common to all – everyone is trained in a particular craft such as processing wool, linen making, masonry, metal working or carpentry. There is no other kind of work that occupies any significant number. Their mode of dress is the same throughout the island and through all stages of life, except for distinctions between the sexes and between the married and the single. By no means unattractive, it's practical for physical activity and adapts to hot or cold weather; each family, as I say, makes its own garments.

Everyone – and that is not just the men but the women as well – learns one of the approved crafts. As the weaker sex

the women take on the lighter ones, for the most part working wool and flax; the more strenuous crafts are entrusted to
the men. The majority of children are brought up in the occu-
pation of their father, for almost all of them are drawn to it
by nature, but if someone is drawn to another craft he's
adopted into a family that practises it, care being taken both
by his father and by the authorities to check that he is placed
with a sober and reliable householder. Moreover, if someone
has mastered one trade and desires to learn another, this is
allowed in the same way. When he has mastered both he follows the one he prefers, unless the city has need of one more
than the other.

The principal and almost sole function of the syphogrants
is to oversee and ensure that no one sits around idle but that
everyone works diligently at their craft; at the same time, no
one has to be worn out like a beast of burden, toiling from
dawn to nightfall. Such an abject state is worse than slavery,
and yet it's the common fate of workers just about everywhere,
except among the Utopians.[9] Out of the twenty-four equal
hours into which they divide day and night they allow just six
to work: three hours before noon when they go to lunch, after
which they allow two hours of the afternoon to a siesta, then
three further hours of work are concluded with supper. Count-
ing the first hour after midday as one o'clock, they retire to bed
at about eight and sleep for eight hours.

The spare time between working, sleeping and eating is left
to the preference of the individual, not to fritter away in high
living or idleness but to pursue some chosen interest distinct
from their usual work. Most of them employ these intervals of
leisure in intellectual pursuits, for it's the regular practice to
have public lectures daily before dawn; only those who have
been marked out for literary studies are required to attend, but
a great number – men and women from every calling – go along
as well to hear one or other of the lectures, depending on their
interests. But should anyone prefer to devote this time to their
craft, as is the case with many who aren't drawn to speculative
studies, this isn't discouraged: rather, it's approved as useful to
the commonwealth.

After supper they pass one hour in recreation, in their gardens in the summer or in their communal dining halls during winter. There they either play music or spend the time in conversation. They know nothing of playing with dice, or similar empty and harmful games, but they do have two games not unlike chess. The first is a mathematical combat, in which one number captures another; the second is a game in which the vices line up in battle against the virtues. The latter cleverly shows how the vices clash among themselves but combine against the virtues; then, next, which vices confront particular virtues, how they attack them openly by force or undermine them indirectly by cunning; and further, by what means of defence the virtues resist the onslaught of the vices or by what devices they elude their stratagems. Finally, by what means one side or the other achieves victory.

But, just in case you get the wrong idea, this is the point at which we need to look more closely into one specific issue. Since they give just six hours to work, you might expect the consequence to be a shortage of necessities. This is far from being the case: the time so allotted is adequate to provide not only a sufficiency but more than enough of the essentials – and even some of the comforts – of life. You'll appreciate why this is so if you reflect on how large a part of the population in other nations passes the time in idleness. For a start, there are most of the women, and they make half of the total; or, where the women do work, the majority of the men who are snoring in their place. Add to this the swarm of priests and so-called religious, as slothful as they are numerous. Add further all the rich, especially the landowners who are generally known as gentlemen or lords, and include their retainers – those swashbuckling, parasitical dregs. Finally, count in those fit and sturdy beggars who use sickness as a cover for sloth. You will certainly find that all the things that meet the requirements of human life are produced by far fewer hands than you had supposed.

Consider now how few of those who do work are engaged in essential tasks, for the simple reason that when money is the measure of all things, futile and unnecessary trades are bound to be practised, just to meet the demands of luxury and

indulgence. Even if the existing labour force were to be redirected to those few trades which cater for the requirements
(equally few) that nature demands for a healthy and comfortable life, the result would be such over-production that prices
would fall and the workers be unable to make a living. But if all
those now engaged in useless trades, plus that whole mob of
loafing idlers (any one of whom consumes twice as much as the
workers who supply his needs), were assigned some useful
tasks, you can easily see how just a little time would be enough
to supply all that human necessity and convenience needs – and
pleasure, too, provided that it is genuine and accords with
nature.

The experience of Utopia makes this crystal clear. For there,
in an entire city with all its adjacent countryside, only five hundred are exempted from all the men and women whose age and
fitness make them liable for work. This includes the syphogrants
who by law are released from manual labour; in practice, however, they don't exempt themselves, so that they can more easily
draw the others to work by their example. The same exemption
is also enjoyed by those who, having been recommended by the
priests and elected in a secret ballot by the syphogrants, are
permanently freed by the community to pursue higher studies.
If one of these scholars disappoints the hopes placed in him, he
is sent back to the ranks of the workers. By contrast, it turns
out not infrequently that a manual worker devotes his leisure
time so earnestly to study that he is released from his craft
and promoted to the ranks of the scholars. From this class of
intellectuals are drawn ambassadors, priests, tranibors, and
ultimately the governor himself, known in their ancient tongue
as Barzanes but nowadays as Ademus. Since virtually the whole
of the remaining population is neither idle nor engaged in useless trades, it's easy enough to grasp how they get so much
profitable work done in only a few hours.

There is a further advantage to be added: in most of the
essential crafts there is less to be done than among other nations.
For a start, everywhere else the construction and repair of
buildings demand the unremitting labour of a large workforce,
because what a father puts up his spendthrift son allows to fall

down bit by bit, and as a result what could have been maintained at a reasonable cost has to be restored at great expense by the next owner. And what's more, when a house has cost one man a huge outlay, someone else with pretensions to taste may disdain it, let it crumble, and then build another on a different site for no less expense. But among the Utopians, where everything is well ordered and the public good rules, a new building on a new site is a very rare event; not only are they quick to repair existing damage but they even anticipate potential problems. So it is that their buildings last for a very long time with the minimum of attention, and the builders sometimes have so little to do that they are set to shaping timber and squaring stone against future needs so that the work can be done more swiftly.

Then consider how little effort their clothing demands. First of all, at work, they are dressed in practical garments of leather or skin which last seven years. When they go out in public they cover these rough clothes with a cloak, identical throughout the island and the colour of undyed wool. It follows that they not only need much less woollen cloth than is required anywhere else, but that which they do use is much less expensive. Yet they make wider use of linen cloth since it is made with less labour. In linen the whiteness is prized, and in wool cleanliness, but they set little store by fineness of weave. Thus while in other places a man can scarcely survive without four or five woollen gowns of various colours and silk shirts to match – and as many as ten with the more modish – there everyone is content with one that lasts for two years. There's no reason why anyone should want more, for if he had more he wouldn't be any better shielded against the cold, nor would he seem a jot more in fashion.

So, with everybody engaged in useful occupations and these in turn requiring less labour, there is such abundance of everything that they sometimes allocate great numbers of workers to restore the public roads, should any be in disrepair. And often, when there is no call even for this kind of work, they officially declare a shorter working day. For the magistrates never compel their citizens to undertake pointless labour against their will,

seeing that the whole aim of their social order is that all citizens
should be free, as far as public requirements allow, to turn from
the servitude of the body and dedicate themselves to the freedom and cultivation of the mind. For in that they consider the
true happiness of life to reside.

Social Relations

This would seem to be the place to give some account of the
forms of social life – how the citizens behave to one another,
and their manner of distributing goods. To begin, then, each
city is made up of households, consisting for the most part of
blood relatives. For the women, once they have grown up and
married, transfer to their husbands' households; male children
and grandchildren, on the other hand, remain in the household
and are subject to the oldest member, unless he shows signs of
senility, in which case the next in order of age takes his place.
So as to ensure that the cities are neither under- nor overpopu-
lated, care is taken that each household (there are six thousand
of them in each city, leaving aside the rural districts) has no
fewer than ten or more than sixteen adults.[10] Naturally, there is
no way to fix the number of young children. This optimum
figure is easily maintained by transferring members from a
household with too many to one with too few. But if the numbers in a city exceed the fixed level, the overflow is used to
make up the shortfall in under-populated cities. And if it should
happen that the total population of the island expands beyond
its projected quota, citizens are enrolled from any of the cities
and they establish a colony subject to their own laws on the
neighbouring mainland, wherever the native population has
redundant and untilled land. The natives, should they wish to
participate, are included. Freely sharing the same way of life
and the same rules of conduct, the two groups easily bond
together, much to their mutual profit. For by their enterprise
the Utopians make that land which previously seemed poor
and barren yield plenty for all. But all those who refuse to live
under their laws the Utopians drive out of the territory that

they claim, making war on those who resist. For they view it as an entirely just cause for war when those who possess a territory leave it idle and unproductive, denying use and possession to others who, by the law of nature, ought to be fed by it. If by any mischance the population of one city drops so far that it cannot be restored without reducing other cities below strength (something, they say, that has happened only twice in their entire history as the result of a devastating plague), then they make up the numbers by recalling people from the colonies; they would rather allow the colonies to founder than that any of the island cities should be weakened.

But let's get back to the common life of the citizens. As I said, the oldest male rules each household; wives serve their husbands, children their parents and younger people generally their seniors. Each city is divided up into four equal districts, and in the middle of each district is situated a market place for every kind of commodity; the products of all the households are brought there and stored in warehouses, each commodity in its specific place. From these the head of each household searches out whatever he or his household needs and carries away their requirements without any payment or recompense. After all, why should anything be denied him? There is more than enough of everything, and there is no fear that anyone will take more than they really need. Why should anyone be suspected of taking too much when he can be sure that he will never run short of anything? For it is certain that among all living creatures greed and aggression are driven by the fear of want; only among mankind are they stirred by pride, which considers it glorious to outshine others by flaunting one's possessions, a kind of vice that is wholly alien to the Utopian way of life.

Set out on the market place which I have just mentioned are the food stalls, on which are displayed not only vegetables, fruit and breads, but also fish, meat and poultry, these latter being prepared at designated places outside the city where running water can remove all the blood and waste. The meat is fetched from these sites where it is slaughtered and cleaned by bondsmen. The Utopians won't allow their own citizens to become

inured to the butchery of animals: it's their view that such practices gradually deaden the sense of compassion, the most
essential of human feelings.[11] They also forbid the carrying of
anything unclean or noxious into the city in case the air might
be contaminated and spread disease.

Then, in each residential block stand spacious halls, all at the
same distance from each other and each one known by a particular name, and here the syphogrants reside. Thirty households
are assigned to take their meals in common at each hall, that is
to say, fifteen from either side along the row.[12] The stewards of
all these halls gather in the market at a designated time and
apply for rations in accordance with their numbers, but priority is given to the sick, who are cared for in public hospitals.
There are four of these situated around the periphery of each
city, just outside the city walls, and they are built on the scale of
a small town. This is so that the sick, however numerous, won't
be squeezed into overcrowded wards, and so that those suffering from contagious diseases that might spread from one to the
other can be isolated. The hospitals are so well planned and
equipped with everything necessary to restore health, the care
provided is so gentle and attentive, and the presence of the most
skilled medical specialists so constant that while no one is sent
there against their will, scarcely a sick person in the entire city
would not rather be nursed there than at home.

When the steward of the sick has received the food prescribed by their physicians, then the best of the remainder is
distributed fairly among the halls according to the numbers in
each, except that special regard is paid to the governor, the high
priest and the tranibors, as well as to ambassadors and foreign
visitors – should there be any, for they are few and infrequent.
In the case of the latter, when they do come special quarters,
fully equipped, are provided for them. At the times set for the
morning and evening meals a trumpet call summons the
syphograncy together, except for those confined to bed in hos-
pital or at home. Once the halls have been supplied, no one is
prevented from taking home food from the market, for they
recognize that this would not be done without good reason.
For while there's no specific rule against eating at home, no one

does so from choice since it's regarded as rather unsocial; what's more, it would be sheer folly to go to all the effort of preparing an inferior meal when a rich and sumptuous one can be had in the adjacent hall.

In this hall the dirty and more arduous tasks are carried out by slaves. But responsibility for planning the meal and preparing and cooking the food rests exclusively with the women, each family taking it in turn. Depending on the numbers eating, they sit down at three or more tables: the men are placed with their backs to the wall and the women are on the outside. This is so that if one of them feels unwell, as often happens in pregnancy, she can get up discreetly and slip out to the nursery. For there is a special dining room set aside for nursing mothers and their children, provided with a fire and a constant supply of clean water. There are also cradles so that they can lay down their babies, or if they wish unwind them from their swaddling clothes in order to play by the warmth of the fire. Each child is nursed by its own mother, unless death or sickness intervenes. In that event the wives of the syphogrants quickly seek out a substitute. This presents no difficulty: a woman in a position to do so will offer herself more willingly for this than any other duty since her tender-heartedness is praised by all, and the child accepts the nurse as its natural parent.

All children under the age of five sit together in the nurses' chamber. The other minors, among whom they include all those of either sex not yet of marriageable age, either wait at table or, if they are not yet old and strong enough for that, stand by in complete silence. Both of these feed on whatever is passed to them by those seated and have no separate time allotted for their meals. The syphogrant and his wife sit at the middle of the high table: this is the most honourable place from which the entire company can be viewed since it's set at the raised end of the hall, crosswise to the other tables. By them sit two of the eldest residents, for seating is always arranged in groups of four. However, should there be a temple within the district, the priest and his wife sit with the syphogrant so that they can preside. On either side of them are placed younger people, then older again, and so on round the hall, so that those of a similar age are together but are still mixed with those of a different age. The point of this, so they say, is that the sober manner of the elderly and the respect they inspire will inhibit the younger ones from improper chatter or gestures, seeing that they are on all sides and nothing can be said or done that escapes their notice.

The serving dishes aren't passed straight down the tables in sequence from the top but first the older people, who are seated in places of honour, are offered the choicest food, and then the others are given equal portions of what is left. If they feel like it, the elders may share with those seated near them the delicacies that weren't in sufficient supply to go all round; in this way seniority is duly respected but everyone shares the benefits.

All meals, whether lunch or dinner, begin with some reading on a moral theme, but it's kept short in case it wearies the listeners, and using it as a basis the elders initiate some suitable conversation, neither too ponderous nor facetious. They don't monopolize the meal-time with long-winded talk but freely listen to their juniors and deliberately draw them out so that they can gauge each one's aptitude and disposition as these are revealed in the informality of dinner-table exchanges.

While their lunches are hurried, their dinners are more elaborate, seeing that the former is followed by work, but dinner by sleep and a night's rest, which they regard as good for the digestion. No dinner passes without music, and there is no shortage of sweets in the dessert course. They burn spices, sprinkle perfume and omit nothing that can delight the company, for they are rather inclined to the view that no kind of pleasure is forbidden, provided that no harm comes of it.[13] This, then, is the manner of life they follow in the city; but country-dwellers, who are more scattered, all eat in their homes. No rural household goes short of food as all that's consumed by the city-dwellers originates with them anyway.

On the Travels of the Utopians

When someone feels the desire to visit friends in another city, or even just to look around the place, he can easily obtain leave

from his syphogrant and tranibor, unless some practical necessity hinders it. He sets out as one of a group, armed with a
letter from the governor that both grants them liberty to travel
and specifies a date for their return. A wagon is provided, along
with a public slave to drive the oxen and look after them, but,
unless the company includes women, they forego the wagon as
more trouble than it's worth. Throughout their travels they
carry nothing with them, yet they are never short of anything
because everywhere they are at home. If they linger in a place
more than one day, each of them practises his trade there, and
is warmly received by his fellow workers.

Should anyone wander outside his own district without leave
and be caught without the governor's pass, he's regarded with
contempt, brought back like a fugitive and severely punished. If
he attempts it a second time he's sentenced to slavery. On the
other hand, if anyone wishes to wander around the territory
belonging to his own city he isn't prevented, provided that he
has the approval of his father and the consent of his wife. Wherever he ends up in the country, he receives no food until he has
completed the work adequate to a morning or an afternoon
shift; subject to this proviso, he can go where he likes within
the bounds of the territory since he is just as useful to the city
there as if he were actually at home.

You can see now that there is never any opportunity to waste
time or be idle: no wine-bars, ale-houses or brothels; no chances
for seduction, no dark corners or furtive encounters.[14] Being
always in the public gaze, it's inevitable that they either get on
with their customary work or enjoy their leisure in some not
unsuitable manner. Such social habits necessarily result in an
abundance of produce, and since this is distributed equally
among all, it follows that no one can be afflicted with poverty
or forced to beg.

In the senate at Amaurot (to which, as I said earlier, each city
sends three representatives every year), they first establish
where there's been a plentiful harvest and where there's been a
poor one, and speedily remedy one district's shortfall with
another's surplus. This transfer is entirely gratuitous: those who
give get nothing in return from the recipients. But those who

have donated to one city from their resources, seeking nothing in return, then receive their particular requirements from another city to which they give nothing. In this way the whole island is like a single household.

After they have made adequate provision for themselves – which they reckon in terms of two years' supply in order to allow for the uncertainties of the year to come – the Utopians export a great quantity of those items in which they have a surplus, things like grain, honey, wool, flax, timber, scarlet and purple dye-stuffs, hides, wax, tallow and leather, as well as livestock. A seventh part of all these they donate to the poor of the country receiving them, and the remainder they sell at a fair price. Such foreign trading enables them to acquire not only those goods which they lack at home (iron is about the only thing in that category) but also a great quantity of silver and gold. By long continuance of this kind of exchange they have built up quite incredible reserves of these precious metals. So, as things stand, they aren't much concerned whether they sell for cash or for credit, and most of the payments they receive come as the latter. However, in all dealings based on credit, they never accept the undertakings of individuals but require the written guarantee of the foreign city. When the day for settlement arrives, the city collects the money from the private debtors and places it in the treasury; it then enjoys the use of it until the Utopians ask for payment. In practice, they seldom claim most of it, since they think it is hardly just to take something that is of no use to them away from those who actually need it. Nonetheless, should circumstances require, they do insist on payment, either in order to lend to some other nation, or because they are at war. For this is the sole purpose for which they hold so much treasure at home: to provide security against major threats or unforeseen emergencies. In particular, they use it to pay inflated rates to foreign mercenaries, whom they would much rather expose to danger than their own citizens, knowing full well that with adequate cash inducements even their enemies can be bought or set at odds among themselves, whether by treacherous means or open conflict.

So it is for this reason that they hold such a store of treasure, but not in the customary way. Indeed, I'm a bit hesitant about describing quite how they do keep it for fear that you won't believe me, a fear that's all the stronger since, if I hadn't seen it with my own eyes, I would have had the greatest difficulty myself in accepting it from anyone else's account. For it's almost invariably the case that the further removed something is from the common practice of the listeners, so much the harder is it for them to credit it. All the same, a perceptive observer, seeing that all the Utopians' other customs are so unlike ours, won't be surprised that their use of gold and silver matches better their manner of life than ours. For a start, they don't use money themselves but hold it back against an emergency that may or may not ever happen, and in the meantime they treat gold and silver (from which money is minted) in such a way that no one will value them above their intrinsic worth. On this basis anyone can see that they are both far inferior to iron and, heaven knows, people can no more live without iron than they could without fire or water. By contrast, nature has allotted no function to gold or silver that we can't do without; only human folly has rated them as precious because they are rare. Nature, for her part, like an indulgent mother, has placed all wholesome things, like air, water and earth itself, within our reach; those that are vain and unprofitable she hides away in inaccessible places.

Now in Utopia, if these precious metals were kept locked in some tower, it might be rumoured (given the foolish ingenuity of the mob) that the governor and senate were deluding the people in order to serve their own ends. If, on the other hand, they were to be made into drinking vessels and other products of the goldsmith's art and the need then arose for them to be melted down for soldiers' pay, the Utopians recognize that people would be extremely reluctant to be parted from objects in which they had begun to take delight. To counter these difficulties they have worked out a scheme that fits in with all their other customs but stands completely at odds with ours, seeing that we make such a fuss about gold and hoard it so carefully. Unless you see it in operation it seems quite incredible.

For while they eat and drink from vessels made of earthenware or glass, elegantly designed but cheap, they use the gold and silver to manufacture chamber pots and other sordid receptacles for use not only in the public halls but also in private homes.[15] What's more, the chains and heavy fetters used to restrain slaves are made from the same metals. And to round it off, those who are marked out for public shame on account of some crime have gold rings dangling from their ears, gold rings on their fingers, gold chains round their necks, and even their heads are crowned with gold.

Thus they contrive in every way to bring gold and silver into low esteem. The outcome is that if it were ever necessary for all these metals to be taken away, something that most other nations regard as the equivalent of disembowelling, no one in Utopia would feel it more than the loss of a penny.

They collect pearls from the seashore, and also diamonds and rubies from some of the rocks, but they don't search for them. Any that they pick up by chance they polish and use to adorn the younger children. In their early days the children delight in such ornaments and show them off, but when they have grown up a bit, and see that only juveniles go in for such trinkets, they discard them – not from parental pressure but from self-respect, much as our children when they grow up throw away their marbles, their lockets and their dolls.[16]

Just how customs so at variance with those of other nations can generate different attitudes has never struck me more forcibly than in the case of the Anemolian ambassadors. These arrived in Amaurot while I was there, and since they came to discuss matters of importance three citizens from each city had assembled in anticipation of their arrival. All the ambassadors from neighbouring lands, who had been in Utopia before and were familiar with local customs, realized that extravagant dress won no credit there: silk was held in contempt and gold regarded as a sign of disgrace. Consequently they were accustomed to attend dressed as simply as possible. But the Anemolians, who came from further away and had fewer contacts with the Utopians, hearing that they all dressed alike in the same simple fashion, made the assumption that they possessed no more than they actually put on. Being themselves proud rather than wise, they resolved to adorn themselves with a magnificence worthy of the gods and to dazzle the eyes of the wretched Utopians with the splendour of their attire.

Accordingly, the three ambassadors made their entry, attended by a retinue of a hundred attendants, all dressed in parti-coloured attire and many of them in silk. The ambassadors themselves, being from the nobility at home, wore cloth of gold, with great chains of gold, as well as gold rings on their fingers, and to top all this, glittering strings of pearls and gems hung on their caps. In brief, they were decked out with just those items which are used in Utopia to punish slaves, shame malefactors or amuse children. It was quite a sight to see the way they gave themselves airs as they compared their finery with the dress of the Utopians who had come crowding out onto the streets; equally, it was just as entertaining to see how far they were misled in their hopes and expectations, and how far they were from getting the respect they anticipated. To the Utopian spectators, apart from the small number who had for some good reason visited foreign lands, the whole pompous display seemed shameful: they paid their respects to the lowest members of the embassy as if they had been lords, but the ambassadors themselves, on account of their gold chains, they took to be slaves and passed by without so much as a nod. As for the children who were beyond the age for gems and pearls, at the sight of these glinting in the ambassadors' caps, they kept nudging their mothers and saying, 'Just look at that great booby, mother, still using pearls and jewels as if he were a little boy.' To which the mother would reply, in all seriousness, 'Shush, son, I reckon he's one of the ambassadors' fools.' Others criticized the gold chains as unfit for purpose: they were so thin that a slave might easily snap them and at the same time so loose that he could wriggle out of them at will and, once free, show a clean pair of heels.

Once the ambassadors had spent a few days among the Utopians, they saw great quantities of gold held in contempt, every bit as despised, in fact, as they were prized in their homeland. They saw, too, that more gold and silver went to make the chains and fetters for a single runaway slave than had provided the finery for all three of them put together. So, humbled and with their wings clipped, they put away all the grand apparel in which they had flaunted themselves – especially after they had spoken sufficiently with the Utopians to grasp their customs and attitudes. For the Utopians are amazed that anyone can take delight in the transitory glitter of a tiny jewel or precious stone when he is free to gaze at a star, or even at the sun itself. Equally, they are amazed that anyone can be so mad as to think himself of nobler stock just because he is clothed in finer wool. However finely spun the wool, a sheep wore it first, and remained just a sheep.

Again, they are astonished that gold, which of itself is perfectly useless, is everywhere so highly prized that man, who imposes value on it for his own purposes, is himself valued at a lower rate. So much so that some dimwit with no more understanding than a block of wood, and as vicious as he is stupid, can hold under his thrall many good and wise men for the simple reason that a great pile of gold coins has come his way. Yet if some twist of fortune or some trick of the law (which is just as apt as fortune to turn things upside-down) should transfer the gold to the lowest creature in his household, in next to no time he'd be the servant of his servant, just like an appendage to the cash. But what shocks them and disgusts them even more is the folly of those who virtually worship the rich, even when they owe them nothing and have no obligation to them, simply because they are rich.[17] Yet they know all too well that they are so tight-fisted and niggardly that not one penny out of that hoard of money will ever come their way.

The Utopians derive these and comparable attitudes in part from their upbringing, being raised in a society whose customs are far removed from idiocy of this sort, and in part from instruction and reading. For though in each city there are only a few who are exempted from manual work to pursue full-time study (those, that is, who reveal from an early age exceptional ability and marked intelligence, along with a natural propensity for the liberal arts), every child is introduced to literary studies. What's more, a good portion of the population, both men and women, devote those hours that are free from manual labour to literature.

They master the various disciplines in their own language, which is neither restricted in its vocabulary nor unattractive to the ear, and conveys the workings of the mind as faithfully as any. Much the same language is used throughout that part of the world, though subject to local corruptions. Prior to our arrival, they hadn't even heard of any of those philosophers whose names are so celebrated among us, yet in music, dialectic, arithmetic and geometry they have progressed as far as our ancient authors. While they equal the ancients in most things, they fall far short of the inventions of our modern logicians. In fact, they haven't even arrived at one of those subtle rules about restrictions, amplifications and suppositions that our youth study in the *Parva logicalia*.[18] What's more, they are so far from competence in handling second intentions that none of them could see 'man-in-general',[19] even though we pointed him out with our fingers and (as you are well aware) he's colossal, bigger than any giant. Despite this, they are highly skilled in charting the course of the stars and the motion of the planets; indeed, they have cunningly devised a variety of instruments by which they calculate with remarkable accuracy the course and position of the sun and moon, and the other stars that can be seen in their sector of the heavens.

As for the conjunctions and oppositions of the planets and that fraudulent nonsense about divination by the stars, they haven't even dreamt about it. From long experience in observing conditions, they can forecast rains, winds and changes in the weather. But as for the causes of such things, or the action of tides in the sea or its salinity, or, above all, the origins and nature of the heavens and earth: up to a degree they treat these issues in the manner of our ancient philosophers, even to the extent of disagreeing with each other. Consequently, when they put forward new theories, they differ from the ancients but reach no final consensus among themselves.

In moral philosophy they carry on just the same debates as we do. They investigate the goods of the mind and of the body and those goods external to us, and then whether the term

'good' fits with all three or is just applicable to the mind.[20] They
discuss virtue and pleasure, but their paramount concern is
with human happiness and whether it consists of one thing or
many. Here they seem to tip the scales a bit too much in favour
of the advocates of pleasure, as they locate in this the whole or
the most important part of human happiness.[21] And what will
surprise you even more is that they seek support for this indulgent opinion from religion, which is solemn and austere – you
might almost say gloomy and inflexible. For they never discuss
happiness without joining to the rational arguments of philosophy certain principles drawn from religion; without these they
consider mere reason alone to be weak and inadequate for the
investigation of true happiness. These are the sort of principles
involved: that the soul is immortal,[22] and by the goodness of
God destined to happiness; then, that after this life our virtues
and good acts will be rewarded and our shameful acts punished. Although these tenets are essentially religious, they judge
that reason leads us to believe in them and assent to them; they
declare without hesitation that were these principles put aside
then no one would be so crass as not to feel obliged to chase
after pleasure, right or wrong. You'd only have to take care not
to let a lesser pleasure block a greater one, and to avoid any
pleasure that carries painful consequences. They consider that
you'd have to be really demented to tread the path of harsh and
demanding virtue, not only dismissing life's pleasures but actually putting up with pain from which you can expect no benefit.
For what benefit could there be if, after death, you gain nothing
for having spent your life without pleasure, in other words,
miserably?

Mind you, they think that happiness is not to be found in
just any kind of pleasure but only in good and proper pleasure;
for virtue draws our nature to this as to its highest good (though
one dissenting view sees the ground of happiness in virtue
itself[23]). Virtue they define as living in accord with nature, God
having created us to that end: anyone who responds to the
promptings of reason as to what we should seek or what we
should avoid is following the lead of nature. In the first place,
reason stirs us to love and reverence the majesty of God, to

whom we owe both our being and our capacity for happiness. Secondly, it impels us to live a life as free of trouble and as full of joy as possible, while assisting everyone else to achieve that goal on account of the common nature we share. For there's never been an advocate of virtue and enemy of pleasure so grim and inflexible who won't, as he directs you on to toils, vigils and self-denial, urge you at the same time to do your utmost to relieve the poverty and misfortune of others. He'll regard such solidarity and mutual support as worthy of praise in the name of humanity, since it is essentially humane (and no other virtue is more fitting to human beings than that) to relieve the troubles of others, to wipe away their sorrows and bring them back to an agreeable, that is a pleasurable, life. Why, then, shouldn't nature prompt us to do the same for ourselves? For either a joyful life, one full of pleasure, is a bad thing: in which case, not only should you not help anyone to it, but you should actively deprive them of it as noxious and harmful. Or else, if you are not only allowed but even obliged to assist others to such a joyful life, then why not first of all do it for yourself? You should be no less generous to yourself than you are to others.[24]

Consequently, they argue, nature herself prescribes for us a joyful life, that is to say one of pleasure, as the final end of all our actions, and to live in accord with her precepts is their idea of virtue. But as nature prompts us to help each other to a happier life (which she does rightly, since no one is so elevated above the common level of humanity as to be the sole focus of her attention, and she cherishes equally all those whom she binds together in a common mode of being), so she counsels us again and again not to pursue our own advantage at the expense of others. Accordingly they hold that it isn't only agreements between private parties that should be observed, but also those public laws which control the distribution of vital supplies and the raw materials of pleasure, whether these are promulgated by a good ruler or ratified by the common consent of a free people without any coercion or trickery. When such laws are in place, it's only sensible to look after your own interests. To further the public interest as well shows a high sense of duty, but to snatch away the pleasure of others in pursuit of your own is criminal. In contrast, to deprive yourself of some pleasure in order to give it to another is a humane and generous act that never fails to give greater returns than it costs. It is repaid by reciprocal benefits, as well as by the sense of having acted well, and the mind gets more pleasure from the affection and goodwill of those you have helped than your body could have gained from the pleasure you sacrificed. Finally, as religion easily persuades any well-disposed mind, God will compensate the loss of brief and uncertain pleasures with joys without measure or end. So it is that, after thorough investigation of the issue, they conclude that our actions, and even the virtues they bring into play, are all directed to pleasure as their final end and fulfilment.

They designate as pleasure every movement or condition of body or mind that gratifies a natural inclination. Certainly, it's no accident that they give this emphasis to natural desire, for not only our senses but right reason[25] too points us towards whatever is naturally pleasurable: something which is achieved without injury to others, which does not cancel a greater pleasure, and which carries no unpleasant consequences. As a result they conclude that those unnatural things which, as by some grotesque conspiracy, people picture to themselves as delights (as if things could be altered in nature by a change of name) contribute nothing to happiness but effectively hinder it. Once these specious delights have infiltrated the mind they leave no room for genuine gratification but flood it with a false notion of pleasure. For there are many things which of their nature contain nothing whatever of delight but rather a great deal of bitterness, and yet through the perverse attraction of false desires these aren't just held to be the greatest of pleasures but numbered among the principal reasons for living.

Among the devotees of spurious pleasure they place some whom I've mentioned already, those that is who regard themselves as superior people because they wear superior clothes. In this they err twice over, for they are no less misguided about their clothes than they are about themselves. If you consider the practical use of a garment, why is a fine-textured weave any

better than a coarse one? And yet they strut around and believe
that the fabric adds not a little to their own worth, as if they
were singled out by nature herself rather than by their own
folly. Consequently, decked up in their fancy attire, they demand
as of right honours such as they would never have dared to
hope for in humbler dress, and they are indignant if some dis-
tracted passer-by fails to show them proper deference.

Taking things a bit further, doesn't it betray just the same
kind of folly to be preoccupied with empty and meaningless
honours? What genuine pleasure can you get from someone
else's uncovered head or bent knee? Will it cure the ache in your
own knees, or cool the fever in your own brain? Included in the
mirage of counterfeit pleasures are those who cheerfully rave
and flatter themselves with the reputation of nobility, congratu-
lating themselves on their descent from a long line of wealthy
ancestors (wealth being the only basis for nobility these days)
and, in particular, on their extensive estates. Yet they don't consider themselves any less noble if their ancestors haven't left
them an inheritance, or if they have squandered the lot.

Along with these the Utopians include a category that I
touched on before, people who are obsessed with jewels and
precious stones and imagine themselves to be as happy as a
god if they obtain an exceptional specimen, especially if it happens to be the kind that is currently in fashion – for a stone
won't hold the same value in all places and times. They'll only
make an offer if a jewel is removed from its gold setting and
exposed to view, and even then only if the dealer swears an
oath and gives security that it's the real thing, so afraid are
they that their eyes will be deceived by a fake. Yet why should
a counterfeit give any less pleasure to your sight when your
eyes can't tell the difference from the genuine article? Heaven
knows, they should carry the same worth for you as they
would for a blind man.

Now what about those who hoard riches, not so as to put
them to use but just to enjoy gazing at them? Do they experience a true pleasure, or are they simply deluded by a false one?
Or those with the contrary vice, who hide away the gold they
will never use and probably never see again, in effect losing it

through their fear of loss? For what else is it to deny yourself –
and conceivably everyone else too – its use by sticking it back in
the ground? Yet once the treasure is hidden, you exult as though
you had attained true serenity of mind. Suppose now that someone stole it, without your finding out, and then ten years later
you died; during that ten years when you outlived the loss of the
money, what difference did it make to you whether it was safe
or stolen? In either case it was equally useless to you.

To these bogus delights they add playing at dice (a craze they
know from report rather than experience), as well as hunting
and hawking. Where, they ask, is the pleasure in throwing dice
on a gaming table? Even if it did hold some appeal, that would
soon grow tedious from repetition. What charm, rather than
disgust, can there be in listening to the barking and howling of
dogs? Why should anyone get more excitement from seeing a
dog chase a hare rather than a dog chasing a dog? You get
plenty of coursing in both these cases, if that's what delights
you. But if it's slaughter that attracts you, the anticipation of
witnessing a kill, then the spectacle of a weak, timid and inof-
fensive little hare being ripped apart by a fierce and savage
hound ought rather to inspire pity. That's why the Utopians,
who regard the whole business of hunting as unsuitable for free
men, have passed it all over to the butchers, and they – as I said
before – are slaves. They rate hunting as the meanest of the
butchers' duties, the others being both more useful and more
decorous as well as more efficient since they kill animals only
to meet demand, whereas the huntsman seeks only his own
pleasure in the killing and dismembering of some hapless little
beast. They consider that an appetite for such violent scenes of
slaughter, even if it's only of animals, either arises from a cruel
disposition or else, by the continual pursuit of such pleasures,
eventually generates cruelty.[26]

According to popular opinion these, and countless other
activities like them, rate as pleasures; but the Utopians hold
that since there's nothing in them that gratifies nature they
clearly have nothing to do with real pleasure. The fact that they
tickle the senses of the general run of humanity (which seems to
be the function of pleasure) in no way alters Utopian opinion,

for the enjoyment doesn't result from the nature of the act in itself but rather from those false perceptions by which people take bitter things for sweet, much as pregnant women find pitch and tallow sweeter than honey because of their disordered palate. A subjective view, whether distorted by sickness or by social custom, can no more change the essential nature of pleasure than it can anything else.

Those pleasures which the Utopians do admit as genuine they divide into various categories, attributing some to the mind and others to the body. To the mind they allow understanding and that delight which arises from contemplation of the truth. To these they add the recollection of a life well-lived, along with the sure hope of joys to come.

Bodily pleasure they divide into two kinds. The first is that which floods the senses with direct pleasure, either when those organs which have been exhausted by bodily combustion are revived, as with food and drink, or when bodily excesses are expelled. The latter happens when we discharge excreta, engage in sexual intercourse, or relieve troublesome irritation with a rub or a good scratch. From time to time a genuine pleasure arises which isn't concerned with meeting the body's demands or easing its discomforts, but from something that affects and stimulates our senses with a secret but perceptible force and possesses them, as happens in the case of music.

The second category of bodily pleasure they take to be that which consists in a calm and balanced condition of the body, in other words, its maximal state of health unaffected by any disorder. Health itself, if free from pain, gives pleasure, even without the addition of any external stimulus; although it is less obvious and has less impact on the senses than the peremptory desire for food and drink, many consider it all the same to be the greatest pleasure of all. Most Utopians admit it as the foundation and ground of all pleasures, since by itself it can render life tranquil and desirable while in its absence there is no scope whatever for pleasure. Indeed, they regard the absence of pain without the addition of health as a state of torpor rather than enjoyment. The view of those who don't consider stable and uninterrupted health to be a pleasure, since it can only be felt through some external stimulus, they rejected long ago, for they have aired the matter pretty thoroughly among themselves. So today, against such a view, nearly all Utopians agree that health is a primary ingredient of pleasure. Since disease brings pain, they say, which is as unyielding an enemy to pleasure as disease is to health, should not pleasure accompany unalloyed good health? They think it has no relevance whether the pain is the disease itself or a concomitant of it, for either way it comes to the same thing. Certainly, whether health is a pleasure in itself or has pleasure as its necessary accompaniment, like heat to fire, in either case it turns out that those who have sound health cannot fail to have pleasure.

Further, what happens when we eat, they say, is that health, which has begun to falter, takes on food as its ally in the fight against hunger. While our health gradually recovers strength, the process of regaining its customary vigour generates that pleasure by which we are refreshed. And if health takes such pleasure in the fight, won't it rejoice once victory is achieved? When it has eventually recovered its original strength – which was the whole point of the exercise – will it immediately slump into a stupor and fail to recognize and embrace its own good? They view the contention that you can't actually feel health as far from true: for who when fully awake doesn't feel himself to be healthy – except for someone who isn't? Who is so weighed down by dullness or lethargy that he won't admit that health is pleasing and delightful? And what, after all, is delight but pleasure under another name?

In the first place, therefore, they embrace pleasures of the mind, which they regard as paramount, and judge the most important to be those which arise from practice of the virtues and awareness of a good life. As for pleasures of the body, there they award the prize to health. Thus they regard the delights of eating and drinking and things that give a similar kind of gratification as desirable, but only for the sake of health, since they are not rewarding in themselves except as means to check the insidious advance of infirmity. Just as a wise man would sooner keep clear of sickness than find a remedy for it, or put sorrows to flight rather than accept consolation, so, too, it would be better not to need this kind of pleasure at all rather than be relieved by it. If anyone thinks that happiness lies in this sort of pleasure, then he would have to admit that his ideal existence would be one spent in a continuous round of hunger, thirst and itching, with the consequent eating, drinking, scratching and rubbing – which you can see is not only squalid but pathetic. Obviously these pleasures are the lowest of all, just as they are the least pure, since they never occur except in conjunction with their contrary discomforts.[27] So the pleasure of eating is allied to hunger, but with no equal relation, for the pain is the fiercer and lasts longer; in fact, it arises before the pleasure and is only relieved when the pleasure fades too. Thus, except in so far as they are driven by necessity, the Utopians don't rate such pleasures highly. All the same, they do enjoy them, and gratefully acknowledge the tenderness of Mother Nature, who coaxes her offspring with the sweetest delights to do what they would in any case have to do out of strict necessity. How wearisome life would be if such everyday ailments as hunger and thirst had to be countered by drugs and bitter medicines like some other diseases that attack us less frequently.

Beauty, strength and agility they happily cherish as special and pleasing gifts of nature. But as to those pleasures which we receive through the ears, eyes and nose and which nature allocates uniquely to mankind (for no other kind of animate creature contemplates the form and beauty of the universe, or responds to any charm of smell other than to distinguish food, or can discern the harmonious or dissonant intervals of sounds), these, I say, they cultivate as adding savour to life. However, in all pleasures they have this rule, that a lesser enjoyment must not impede a greater one, and no pleasure should give rise to pain – which they think invariably happens if the pleasure is shameful. But they consider it utter madness for anyone to despise bodily grace, to impair his strength, turn agility into lethargy, wear down his body with fasting, damage his health, and treat all other favours of nature with contempt – unless by this neglect of self he can more ardently serve the interests of others or the common good, and in return for his pains hope to receive a greater pleasure from God. Otherwise, to torment oneself, whether for some empty shadow of virtue that does nobody any good or in order to harden oneself against afflictions that may never even occur, is in their eyes absurd, betraying a mind at once cruel to itself and most ungrateful to nature – just as if it were shunning her gifts so as to avoid being in her debt.

These are their thoughts about virtue and pleasure, and they hold that human reason can come no closer to the truth unless some heavenly revelation might inspire people with holier ones.[28] There's no time now to consider whether they are right or wrong in all this, nor is it necessary. I have undertaken to describe their practices, not to defend them. But of one thing I am firmly convinced, that whatever the worth of these principles, you will never find a more admirable people or a happier commonwealth. Physically they are agile and lively, endowed with greater strength than you might expect from their build, though they are by no means stunted. The quality of their soil is variable and the climate is not up to much, but they protect themselves against these conditions by temperate living and remedy the shortcomings of the land by hard work, with the result that there's no place where you will find more prolific crops or herds of cattle, or where people's bodies are more vigorous and resistant to disease. Not only do they carefully perform all the usual routines a farmer needs to follow to improve poor soil by art and industry, but they have also been known to uproot an entire forest by hand to transfer it to another site. This wasn't done in order to increase production but to help with transport, so that wood stocks might be closer to the sea and the rivers, or to the cities themselves, since it takes less effort to convey grain over long distances by land than it does to transport wood.

The people are easy-going, good humoured and intelligent, and enjoy their leisure. They accept physical labour willingly provided that it serves a useful purpose (otherwise they are not keen on it), but in matters of the mind they are tireless. When they had heard from us about the literature and learning of the Greeks – for in Latin there was nothing apart from the historians and poets that seemed likely to impress them – it was amazing to see how eagerly they pressed us to help them master these by giving them lessons. So we began to read with them, initially so that we wouldn't seem to grudge the effort rather than because we hoped that they would get any benefit from it. But when we had progressed a bit, their application swiftly made us see that our efforts would be far from wasted. They copied the forms of letters so easily, pronounced the words so readily, committed them to memory so quickly and recited what they had learned with such accuracy that it seemed to us like a miracle. Admittedly, the majority of our pupils undertook these studies not just of their own accord but also at the command of the senate, having been selected from the ranks of the most talented and mature scholars. So it was that within three years they had mastery of the language, and could read the best authors fluently, provided that there were no corruptions in the text.[29] I have the notion that they picked up the language so easily because it's not unrelated to their own; indeed I suspect that their race derived from the Greeks because their language, which in other respects resembles Persian, retains some traces of Greek in the names of towns and public offices.

When I had embarked on the fourth voyage, I took with me a fair-sized chest of books instead of goods for barter, having determined never to return rather than do so too soon. In consequence they got from me most of Plato's works, and all those of Aristotle, as well as Theophrastus' treatise On Plants,[30] which, to my regret, had been mutilated in a number of places. The latter had been carelessly left lying around during the voyage when a monkey discovered it and playfully ripped out a number of its pages and tore them to shreds. Out of the grammarians they have only Lascaris as I didn't take Theodorus with me, or any dictionary except those of Hesychius and Dioscorides.[31] They are particularly fond of Plutarch's works and are much taken with the wit and sparkle of Lucian.[32] As to poets, they have Aristophanes, Homer and Euripides, as well as Sophocles in the small typeface of Aldus.[33] Of the historians they possess Thucydides and Herodotus, along with Herodian.[34]

As for medical matters, a companion of mine called Tricius Apinatus had brought with him certain brief works by

Hippocrates and the *Microtechne* of Galen,[35] all of which they valued highly. While it's true that there is scarcely a country in the world less in need of medicine, in spite of that nowhere is it held in greater honour, since they regard medical science as one of the most noble and useful parts of philosophy.[36] When they use philosophy to probe into the secrets of nature it seems to them that in addition to deriving a deep pleasure from this activity, they attract the special favour of the author and artificer of nature. They judge that, just like any other artist, he created the wonderful fabric of the world so that mankind (to whom alone he has given this capacity) might gaze on it in contemplation. It follows that he's bound to prefer a careful observer and responsive admirer of his work to someone who gazes like a mindless animal, dumb and unmoved at such an awesome spectacle.

With their natural abilities, the Utopians, once they have been prompted by learning, are wonderfully effective at developing those skills which enhance life. Nonetheless, two things they owe to us: printing and the manufacture of paper – and yet not entirely to us but also in good part to themselves. For when we were showing them books printed on paper by Aldus we spoke a bit about the means for making paper and the technique of printing, but in general terms as none of us had practical experience of either skill, yet with remarkable acuity they at once grasped how to set about it. Where before they had written on parchment, bark and papyrus, they now tried to make paper and print letters, and though their first efforts fell short, by frequent attempts they quickly mastered both and became so successful that if they'd had more of the original Greek texts there would have been no shortage of copies. As it is, they have no more than those I have listed, but of these they have printed thousands.

Anyone who comes to view their country and displays some exceptional talent or has acquired knowledge of many lands from extensive travel can be sure of a welcome – which is why our own arrival was so well received. In fact, they are always happy to hear what's going on around the world. However, few are drawn there for the purposes of trade: after all, what could anyone offer except iron – or gold and silver, which other lands prefer to keep for themselves? Where materials for export are concerned, they think it wiser to carry these themselves rather than rely on others to ship them; in this way they discover more about surrounding peoples and maintain their sea-going skills.

Slaves

The Utopians don't regard prisoners of war as slaves, except for those taken in the campaigns they fight themselves; neither do they enslave the children of slaves, or those they take out of slavery in other lands.[37] Their slaves are either their own people, who have been punished for some shameful act, or, most commonly, foreigners who, for some crime, have been condemned to death in their own cities. They carry off many of the latter, sometimes for a low price but more often for nothing. Slaves of this kind they keep not only constantly at work but also in chains, while those drawn from among their own people they treat more harshly yet, since they judge them to be more reprehensible and to merit severer measures because they couldn't be kept from crime in spite of an admirable education that directed them towards virtue.[38] Another class of slaves is made up of hard-working but impoverished drudges from other nations who freely choose to be slaves in Utopia. They deal fairly with these people, treating them not much less generously than citizens, apart from allocating them a little extra work since they are used to it. Should one of them want to leave, which doesn't occur often, they don't hold him against his will or send him away empty-handed.

As I have already said, they care for the sick with marked tenderness, neglecting no means whatever, whether of medicine or diet, by which they might be restored to health. They comfort those suffering from an incurable disease, sitting and talking with them, and doing all they can to alleviate their pain. If, however, the disease not only is untreatable but also involves intense and unrelieved suffering, then the priests and magistrates counsel the patient. They point out that since he's unequal to the obligations of life and is a heavy burden to himself as well as to others, he has in effect outlived his own death. So, buoyed up with hope for better things, he ought to release himself from this harsh life as from a prison or bed of thorns, or permit others to liberate him from it. This would be a sensible thing to do, since death wouldn't bring an end to pleasures but to suffering; what's more, since he'd be following the counsel of the priests, the interpreters of God's will, it would also be a devout and holy act.[39]

Those who accept these arguments either voluntarily starve themselves to death or, after being drugged, are set free without any awareness of death. But death is not forced on anyone who is unwilling, nor is the care they receive lessened in any degree. Those persuaded to die in this way are treated honourably, but anyone who takes his life without the approval of the priests and the senate is considered unworthy of either burial or cremation, and his body is cast into a swamp, unmarked and dishonoured.

A woman does not marry before the age of eighteen, nor a man before he's four years older than that. Anyone found guilty of illicit sexual relations prior to marriage is severely reprimanded and permanently banned from marriage, regardless of their sex, unless the governor remits the sentence. In addition the father and mother of the household in which the offence took place are exposed to public shame for having fallen short in their duties. They punish this offence so severely because they anticipate that unless people are strictly restrained from casual sex few would undertake marriage, with its lifelong commitment to a single partner and all the other irksome demands which that entails. Then, in choosing marriage partners, they solemnly adopt a practice which struck us as quite grotesque, for the woman – be she virgin or widow – is shown to the suitor by some reliable and trustworthy matron while stark naked; and in the same way, some appropriate man shows the suitor naked to the prospective bride.[40] We laughingly dismissed this custom as quite absurd, but they on their part were astonished at the folly of other nations: for these, when they go to buy a young horse, which only involves a small sum of

money, are so wary that even though the beast is virtually bare
they won't complete the deal until its saddle and rug have been
removed, just in case they might hide a sore. But in the choice
of a marriage partner, which is going to be a cause of either
delight or revulsion for the remainder of their lives, they are so
off-hand that while they leave the rest of her body clothed, they
judge the whole worth of the woman from a mere glimpse of
her face, and on this basis they marry her, storing up a high risk
of conflict should an impediment emerge later. Not everyone is
high-minded enough to focus exclusively on character, and
even in marriages of the wise bodily appeal augments qualities
of mind. It's clear that clothing can hide a deformity so repel-
lent as to turn a man's mind against his wife at the very time
when his body can no longer be lawfully separated from her. If
some such disfigurement occurs after marriage, then you have
to accept the dealings of fate; but beforehand, it's up to the
laws to protect people against deception.

There's all the more reason for them to be careful because they
are the only people in that part of the world to be strictly monog-
amous, and their marriages seldom end except by death, unless it
be on the grounds of adultery or the intolerable behaviour of one
of the spouses. The offended party, in such a case, is granted
leave by the senate to remarry; the guilty one is disgraced and
condemned to a single life. Such cases aside, they find it intolerable that a man should repudiate his wife against her will when
there is no fault on her side, just because of some physical infirmity. For they consider it heartless that anyone should be
abandoned when standing most in need of comfort, and that old
age, which not only brings diseases but constitutes one in itself,
should have to rely on an uncertain and fragile trust.[41]

From time to time it happens that in a married couple spouses
whose temperaments are not well matched encounter other
individuals with whom they might hope to lead a happier life;
in this case they can separate by mutual consent and contract
new marriages, but not without the approval of the senate. For
its part, the senate allows divorce only after its members,
together with their wives, have thoroughly investigated the
case. The procedure is demanding because they recognize that

the easy prospect of a new marriage does little to bolster the love between a married couple. Those who violate the marriage bond are punished with the harshest form of slavery. Should neither of the offenders be single then the injured parties, if they so wish, can repudiate their adulterous partners and marry one another, or someone else of their choosing. Yet if one of them persists in loving his or her ill-deserving partner then the marriage can continue, provided that the innocent one is willing to share the penal servitude of the other; and occasionally it happens that the repentance of one and the devoted loyalty of the other move the governor to pity, and he frees them both. But any repetition of the offence is punished by death.

For all other crimes there is no penalty fixed by law, but the senate determines a punishment appropriate to the seriousness of the offence. Husbands discipline their wives, as parents do their children, unless the offence is so grave that public morality demands some exemplary retribution. For the most part, serious crimes are punished with servitude, since it is considered that this is no less daunting to the guilty and far more profitable to the community than hurrying to be rid of them by immediate execution. For one thing, they contribute more alive than they would dead, and then by their example they provide a lasting warning to others to avoid such crimes. But if they rebel and resist such treatment, then – like wild beasts that can't be controlled by either bars or chains – they are put down. And yet, there is always some hope for those who are patient: once they have been tamed by long punishment, if they show by their contrite manner that they regret their crime more than the punishment it brought on them, then by authority of the governor or by a public vote their servitude can be mitigated or remitted altogether.

Any attempt to entice another to commit a lewd act is liable to just the same penalties as the act itself. With any crime they count a clear and deliberate attempt as equal to the deed; as they see it, failure should offer no mitigation to someone who has done all in his power to commit the offence.

They derive a particular delight from fools and consider it shameful to look down on them; consequently they have no problem about finding their folly amusing; indeed, they think that this works in the best interests of the fools themselves. If someone is so stiff and solemn that he's unmoved either by their antics or their sayings, they don't entrust fools to him, as anyone who gets no profit from a fool, not even entertainment (which is all a fool can offer), is unlikely to handle them with much sympathy. To mock the deformed or maimed is regarded as ugly and disfiguring, not to the individual mocked but to the one who mocks, because like an idiot he's blaming the unfortunate victim for something he can do nothing about. While they think it idle and slovenly to neglect one's natural appearance, they regard the use of cosmetics as affected and even sleazy. Long experience has taught them that no physical charms can make a wife attractive to her husband as effectively as moral integrity and a respectful manner. Certainly, some men are caught by looks alone, but none are held securely except by virtue and loyalty.

They don't only deter people from crime by punishments but they lure them to virtue by official honours, and so in public spaces they set up statues of outstanding men who have served the community well, both to preserve the memory of their deeds and so that their glory might act as a spur and incitement to virtue for future generations.

Any person who adopts devious means to win some public office is banned from all of them. The Utopians lead a sociable life together: no magistrate is ever haughty or overbearing, they are known as 'fathers' and behave as such.[42] The due honour that they enjoy is freely given, not reluctantly conceded. Even the governor himself isn't marked out by robes or a crown but by the sheaf of grain that he carries, just as the insignia of the high priest is the wax candle borne before him.[43]

They have very few laws since their schooling is such that very few are needed. What they strongly deplore about other nations is the way that their countless tomes of laws – and of commentaries on them – all prove inadequate. In their view it is a violation of justice that people should be bound by laws which are either too numerous to be read or too obscure to be understood. More than that, they have no time at all for professional lawyers, those who use artifice to present their case and craftily raise points of law; they think it far better that a man should plead his own case, and relate to the judge exactly what he would have said to his own counsel. In this way there is less scope for misunderstanding, and it's far easier to arrive at the truth: the pleader presents things in his own words, without any fancy input by a lawyer, while the judge carefully weighs each point, and protects the interests of the unsophisticated against the devices of more wily opponents. It's not easy to find anything comparable in other countries, with their intricate tangle of obscure laws, but with the Utopians everyone is a legal expert. For the laws, as I've indicated, are very few, and they regard the most straightforward reading as the most equitable. Indeed, they claim that all laws are promulgated in the first place in order to alert people to their obligations. Now, the subtler an interpretation is, the less impact it will have on people, since only a few will grasp it; while, in contrast, the simpler and more obvious sense of the law is clear to everyone. Otherwise, so far as the general public are concerned (and they make up the mass of mankind and stand most in need of guidance), it would make no difference whether you had no laws at all or, were you to enact any, whether you then interpreted them in such a way that nobody could make head or tail of them without dazzling intelligence and exhaustive scrutiny. The stolid mind of the average man can't cope with such a challenge, and could hardly do so in an entire lifetime that is taken up by the struggle for subsistence.

Encouraged by these admirable qualities, those neighbouring peoples who are independent (for the Utopians have long since liberated many of them from tyranny) willingly apply to them for magistrates, some to serve on an annual basis, some for a period of five years. When these have completed their tour of duty they are escorted home with honour and acclaim, and replaced by new Utopians. It does seem that these countries have made the best possible provision for the general welfare. Since the well-being or ruin of a community hangs on the calibre of its public officials, where could they make a wiser choice than among those who, since they will soon return to their moneyless society, can't be corrupted by bribes, and who, as strangers in that community, are unlikely to be swayed by partiality or factional interests?[44] Wherever these two evils of favouritism and avarice insinuate themselves into men's judgements they at once destroy all justice, which is the strongest guarantee of civil society. The Utopians call those peoples who apply to them for officials 'allies'; others whom they have benefited in various ways they refer to as 'friends'.

Treaties, which other nations are forever validating, violating and renewing, they refuse to make with anyone. What's the point of a treaty, they ask, if nature isn't already a sufficient bond between man and man? If anyone is indifferent to that, what are they likely to care about mere words? They are encouraged in this view by the fact that in their part of the world treaties and alliances between rulers are seldom observed with good faith. In Europe, of course, and most especially in those areas where the Christian faith and its observance prevail, the authority of treaties is everywhere regarded as sacred and inviolable. In part this is due to the justice and virtue of the princes, and in part to the awe and reverence in which the Popes are held. Not only do the latter never take on any obligation that they won't most conscientiously perform, but they command all other princes to hold true to their promises in every way, goading on the reluctant with canonical censures and solemn admonitions. Quite rightly they judge that it would be utterly scandalous if those who are known by the specific title of 'the faithful' were to prove faithless in their dealings.

But in that new world – which could scarcely be further removed from ours by the band of the equator than it is by customs and way of life – no trust is placed in treaties. The more elaborate and solemn the ceremonies by which a treaty is ratified the sooner will it be broken: some defect in the wording can easily be found, which will often enough have been deliberately written in in order that the parties won't be so tightly bound that they can't slide out, making a mockery of both the treaty and their commitment. If such deviousness, or, more plainly, such fraud and deception, were to be detected in private dealings, it would be sternly condemned as sacrilegious and worthy of the gallows, and by the very same people who pride themselves on giving just this sort of advice to princes. As a result it appears that justice is merely a humble and plebeian virtue, far below the dignity of kings, or else that there are two applications of justice: one for the crowd, which shuffles along the ground and never breaks bounds, weighed down with chains; another, the resource of princes, which is more elevated than the common sort and so far freer – nothing is forbidden to them except what they don't want.

I would suggest that the tendency of princes in that part of the world to disregard their treaty obligations is the reason why the Utopians don't make any; perhaps if they lived here they would think otherwise. As it is, they consider that the practice of making treaties at all is regrettable, even when they are faithfully observed, since it implies that men are born as instinctive competitors and enemies who quite properly struggle to obliterate each other, unless treaties prevent it – just as if people separated from one another by some minor barrier like a hill or a stream didn't share a common nature. But beyond that, even when treaties are agreed, they don't really promote friendship since both sides retain the licence to plunder each other, seeing that through lack of foresight in drafting the treaty there are no adequate provisions to prevent it. Against this, the Utopians hold that no one is an enemy if he has caused no actual harm, that the shared bonds of nature are every bit as strong as a treaty, and that men are more effectively drawn together by goodwill than by pacts, by hearts rather than by words.

Military Matters

War they loathe utterly as a bestial activity which is, nonetheless, more incessantly practised by humans than by wild beasts; and in contrast to the customs of nearly all other nations, they regard as inglorious all glory won by means of war.[45] As a consequence, although they devote themselves, women as well as men, to regular military training to ensure that they won't be

incapable of defending themselves when the need arises, they
engage in hostilities with great reluctance. They do so only to
safeguard their own frontiers, or to expel hostile forces from
the territories of their friends, or, in the cause of humanity, to
liberate an oppressed people from tyranny and servitude. But
while they give support to their friends, this is not always defensive but may sometimes be in retaliation for injuries inflicted on
them. They'll only take such a step if they themselves have been
consulted from the outset and have approved the cause, and
then again only if appeals for reparation have been rejected,
and provided that they initiate the hostilities themselves. This
they'll do not only when their friends have been pillaged by
enemy incursions but also, and with greater intransigence,
when their friends' merchants have been subjected to any sort
of mistreatment, wherever it may be, either under the cover of
unfair laws or through the perverse application of sound laws.

It was precisely this that led to the war that the Utopians
waged on behalf of the Nephelogetes against the Alaopolitans,
not long before the time of our visit: certain Nephelogete
merchants residing among the Alaopolitans suffered some
injustice (at least as they saw it) under the pretence of legal
process. Whatever the rights and wrongs of the case, a savage
war ensued, in which the violence and animosity of the con-
tending parties was heightened by the involvement and material
resources of surrounding nations, with the consequence that
some of the most prosperous countries were either destabilized
or severely damaged. One bad thing led to another, and the
sequence was only brought to an end by the surrender and
enslavement of the Alaopolitans. As a result, since the Utopians
were not fighting for their own benefit, the Alaopolitans were
subjected to the Nephelogetes, a people who in their days of
prosperity had been very much their inferiors.

This shows how sharply the Utopians avenge any ill-treatment
meted out to their friends, even in money matters; but this is not
the case where their own interests are involved. So if they are
cheated out of their goods, and provided that no physical harm
has been done, they restrict their anger to placing an embargo on
trade relations with the country in question until compensation

has been paid. This isn't because they have less concern for their own citizens than for their allies, but because they are more concerned about the latter's material loss than their own. What their friends' merchants lose are private assets, and so they feel the pain of the loss more acutely; but in their own case it is only public goods that are lost, and those that are plentiful and even superfluous at home since they wouldn't have been exported otherwise. So the loss affects no individual. For that reason Utopians consider it sheer cruelty to avenge some such offence, which has neither cost the life nor affected the prospects of any of their people, by causing many deaths. But if a Utopian citizen is unjustly wounded or killed anywhere, whether it's the result of official or private action, they send envoys to ascertain the facts and then, unless the culprits are handed over to them, they will not be pacified but immediately declare war. Those responsible for the crime are punished by death or servitude.

A bloody victory doesn't only grieve them, it actually causes them shame, since they regard it as folly to pay too high a price even for the most precious commodities. If they overcome and crush their enemies by artifice and cunning they glory in this, proclaim a public triumph and erect a monument as if for some heroic feat of arms. They argue that in reality they have acted with manliness and courage as often as they conquer by means such as no other animal but man is capable of, that is by the force of intelligence. For, they say, bears, lions, boars, wolves, dogs and all sorts of wild beasts fight with bodily force, and most of them are stronger and fiercer than us, but they are all inferior to us in intelligence and calculation.

Their one aim in going to war is to obtain those objectives which would have prevented hostilities if they had been conceded in the first place. Should this not be possible, they try to inflict such a harsh punishment on those they hold responsible that fear will stop them from attempting anything comparable in the future. These are the goals they set themselves, which they strive to achieve as swiftly as possible, but in such a way as to minimize danger rather than win glory and renown.

Accordingly, as soon as war has been declared, they arrange for proclamations, all authenticated with their official seal, to

be secretly and simultaneously displayed in all the most important public spaces of their enemies' territory. In these they
promise huge rewards to anyone who will do away with the
enemy prince; then they offer lesser, but still significant, rewards
for the heads of such individuals as are also listed. The latter
are those whom they judge, after the prince, to be most responsible for plotting hostile action against them. Whatever reward
they decide for an assassin, they double for anyone who brings
in one of the proscribed individuals alive; in fact, they offer just
the same reward, plus a guarantee of impunity, to any one of
the proscribed who turns against his confederates. In this way,
and in no time at all, their enemies come to distrust all out-
siders, and even among themselves are neither trusting nor
trustworthy, so that they live in extreme dread and no less
danger. Past experience shows how often many of the people
named, and in particular the prince himself, have been betrayed
by those in whom they had placed the greatest trust. Bribes
easily persuade people to any kind of crime, and the Utopians
employ them without restraint. At the same time, mindful of
the risks that they are encouraging others to take, they are careful to ensure that the rewards are proportionate to the danger.
So they promise, and unfailingly deliver, not only immense
amounts of gold but also substantial landed estates in the territory of their friends, to be held with perpetual possession.

This practice of bidding for and buying an enemy is condemned by other nations as the brutality of degenerate minds;
however, the Utopians regard it as judicious and thoroughly
admirable, seeing that it enables them to emerge successfully
from major wars without even fighting, and also as humane
and merciful, since by the deaths of a few guilty men they spare
the lives of many innocent ones on both sides who would
otherwise have died in combat. They feel almost as much pity
for the general mass of the enemy as they do for their own
people, since they know that they don't go to war of their own
volition but are thrust into it by the madness of princes.

If this approach doesn't work, they sow the seeds of discord
and cultivate them by encouraging a brother of the prince or
some member of the nobility to aspire to the throne. And if

internal strife peters out, they stir up their enemies' neighbours and set them on by digging up some ancient claim or other, such as kings always have on hand. Once they have promised practical support for a war they pour in money, but are much more sparing with their citizens: they hold them especially dear, and have so great a bond among themselves that they wouldn't willingly exchange one of their own for the enemy's prince. Gold and silver, though, which they keep for this sole purpose, they spend without stint, seeing that they'll live just as comfortably even if the whole lot is used up. Indeed, as I've said before, over and above their domestic resources, they have a vast store of treasure abroad since many nations are in their debt. So they send to the war mercenaries drawn from all over the place, and particularly from among the Zapoletes.

These people live five hundred miles to the east of Utopia and are savage, uncouth and warlike, happiest among the forests and rugged mountains where they are reared.[46] They are a hardy race, well able to bear heat, cold and bone-crushing toil: oblivious to all refined pleasures, they neglect agriculture, are careless of their dwellings and dress, and only take an interest in their cattle. Most of them live by hunting and pillaging. Born solely for war, they are always seeking an opportunity to wage it and when one is found seize it enthusiastically, flocking out of their country in huge numbers and offering themselves at a cheap price to anyone in need of troops. The only art of living they know is one that procures death. Under the orders of those who pay them they will fight fiercely and with incorruptible loyalty, but they won't commit themselves to serve for any fixed period. Instead, they adopt a side on the strict understanding that should there be a better offer on the next day, even from the enemy, they will align with him; and on the day after that, if a bit more is offered them, they'll go back again. It's unusual for a war to happen in which a good number of them are not serving on both sides, with the result that every day men who are linked by blood and who were the closest of friends when they served together are suddenly divided between opposing sides and clash in battle. Fired by blood lust, oblivious to family ties and the bonds of friendship, they hack at each other, driven to mutual destruction for no other cause than that they have been hired for some pathetic sum by opposing princes. They keep such a tight account of their pay that the addition of a single penny to the daily rate is sufficient to induce them to change sides. They have all too quickly learned avarice, but it does them little good, for what they earn by blood they swiftly squander on wild living of the dreariest sort.

These people fight for the Utopians against all comers, since they pay so much more for their services than anyone else. Indeed, just as the Utopians seek out good men with a view to using them, so they enlist these, the worst of men, in order to misuse them. When the situation demands it they expose the Zapoletes to the greatest dangers, urging them on with the promise of lavish rewards, but the majority never return to claim them. Nonetheless, they pay out all that was promised to the survivors so as to encourage them for the next time. They don't brood too much over the numbers of Zapoletes they have lost since they consider that the human race would owe them a great debt if they rid the world of the offscourings of that unattractive and pernicious people.

After the Zapoletes, the Utopians also make use of troops from the people for whom they are fighting, and then of auxiliary squadrons from other friendly nations. Last of all, they add their own citizens, and choose some man of proven courage from among them to command the entire army. They also place two others under him who, as long as he remains safe, have no official function; but if he is captured or killed, one of them takes over his role, and should anything happen to him, the third one steps in. In this way, in spite of the hazards of war, some threat to the general doesn't throw the whole army into confusion.

Recruitment in each city is drawn from those who have volunteered themselves: no one is pushed into it unwillingly, because they are convinced that anyone who is fearful by nature will not only prove incapable of effective action himself but may even spread panic among his companions. On the other hand, should their own country be attacked, they place all such cowardly recruits (provided they're physically fit), along with more reliable men, on board ships, or here and there along the ramparts, where there's no chance to run away. In this way their sense of shame, the proximity of the enemy and the removal of any hope of escape combine to help them overcome their fear, and often in extreme situations turn it into courage.

But just as no one from among them is forced to participate in a war on foreign territory, so those women who wish to accompany their husbands on campaign are not only not prevented but actively encouraged and even praised for doing so. They march with their husbands and likewise stand with them in line of battle. Moreover, around each soldier are stationed his children and his relatives, whether by blood or marriage, so that those most immediately on hand to help are those prompted by nature to give mutual support. It's deeply shameful for any married person to return home without their partner, or a son without his parent. The outcome is that if it turns to hand-to-hand combat and the enemy stands firm, then the struggle is long and deadly, ending in utter carnage.

They certainly make every effort to avoid being engaged in combat themselves, so long as they can use mercenaries to resolve things on their behalf; but once they can no longer escape direct involvement they're every bit as fearless in action as before they were wise in their efforts to postpone it for as long as possible. Although they're not especially fierce at the first encounter, they gradually fire themselves up as events unfold until they would rather be killed than be driven from the field. Since they can be confident that those at home will be fed, and have no worries about the prospects for their families (a concern that so often compromises the bravest spirit), they are full of courage and dismissive of defeat. Then, their expertise in the arts of war gives them confidence and, on top of this, added strength comes from their positive attitudes – which they have absorbed from childhood through instruction and the sound practices of their commonwealth. So they neither hold life so cheap that they squander it senselessly, nor so precious that they cling on to it shamefully when duty calls them to lay it down.

When the battle is everywhere at its height, a sworn band of carefully picked young men commit themselves to search out

the enemy leader. They go for him openly or set an ambush for
him; from far and near they track him down and attack, adopting an extended wedge-like formation in which tired troops are
continuously replaced by fresh ones. It's seldom that the enemy
leader isn't either killed or captured, unless he takes to flight. If
the victory is theirs there's no slaughter, for they would rather
capture fugitives than kill them; and they never so pursue the
fleeing that they fail to keep one line of battle drawn up under
the standards. So much so, in fact, that if victory is won by this
last line – the rest of the army having been overwhelmed – they
prefer to let the entire enemy force escape rather than run after
the fugitives with their own ranks in disorder. They haven't
forgotten the lessons of the past: on several occasions, with
most of their own army routed and the enemy forces – carried
away by their success – dispersed in pursuit of stragglers, a
small group of Utopians held in reserve have been able to
transform the outcome of the battle by seizing their opportunity
and mounting a sudden counter-attack on their scattered and
undirected adversaries, who, feeling over-confident, had
dropped their guard. In this way they snatched certain and
undoubted victory out of the enemy's hands and, though conquered, in their turn conquered their conquerors.

It's no easy thing to say whether they are most cunning in
setting ambushes or keeping out of them. You'd guess that they
are ready to run away when that's the last thing they have in
mind; by contrast, when they do make that decision, you'd
never imagine they had such a thought. If they feel that inequal-
ity of numbers or the nature of the ground tell against them,
they will either move camp silently by night or slip away by
some comparable ploy; alternatively, if they slip away by day,
they do so gradually and in such good order that it's just as
risky to attack them when they withdraw as when they advance.
They take special care to fortify their camps by means of a
wide, deep ditch, the displaced soil being piled on the inward
side. In all this they don't rely on labourers but the soldiers do
it with their own hands: the entire army is involved, with the
sole exception of armed guards posted in front of the ditch to
repel sudden attacks. Consequently, with so many at work,

they can enclose a large area with awesome fortifications at an amazing speed.

The Utopians use armour that is strong enough to withstand blows and yet hinders movement so little that they can even swim in it. For they include swimming in armour as part of their basic military training. When fighting at long range they use arrows, which are shot with great force and accuracy by both infantry and mounted troops. For close combat they don't use swords but axes, whose weight and sharpness render them lethal, whether used for hacking or thrusting. They are especially ingenious at contriving mechanical instruments of war, but keep them well out of sight just in case, if they were exposed before circumstances required them, they might appear more ludicrous than treatening. In constructing these, their first consideration is to make them easy to transport and manoeuvre on site.

They observe truces agreed with the enemy so scrupulously that they won't break them even if provoked. They will not lay waste enemy territory or burn crops; instead, so far as possible, they try to avoid men or horses trampling them, being well aware that they may use them themselves. They'll do no harm to anyone unarmed, unless he turns out to be a spy. They respect those cities that are surrendered to them, and even leave intact those they have taken by assault, though they execute those individuals who prevented the surrender, and reduce all remaining defenders to servitude. The mass of non-combatants they leave unharmed. If they find any who had argued for surrender, they award them a share in the property of the condemned; the remainder they grant to the auxiliaries, for they never keep any of the booty for themselves.

When a war is over they charge the cost to the conquered rather than to the allies for whose sake they undertook it. On this basis, they take part of their share in money, which they then hold in reserve against future warlike requirements, and part of it in landed estates, which yield substantial income in perpetuity. They have revenues of this kind in many countries, which, having been gradually accumulated for various reasons, now amount to more than seven hundred thousand ducats a

year.[47] To collect them they send out some of their own citizens
to these estates under the title of Quaestors,[48] and these dwell
there in grand style and conduct themselves as major figures in
the community. Nonetheless, there is plenty left to top up the
treasury, unless they choose to lend it to the country concerned.
They do this frequently, until there's some call for the money,
and it's very seldom that they demand the return of the whole
sum. And then, as I've mentioned already, they allot some of
these estates to those who, with their encouragement, have
exposed themselves to danger.

Should any prince take up arms and prepare to invade their
territory, they immediately confront him with a powerful force
beyond their own borders, for they don't like to wage hostilities on their own ground, nor could any crisis be grave enough
to make them admit foreign auxiliaries onto their island.

The Religions of the Utopians

There are various religions, not just throughout the island but
even within individual cities, some honouring the sun as god,
others the moon, yet others one of the planets. There are those
who look up to some man who in ancient times was honoured
for virtue or glory not simply as a god but as the highest god.
But by far the greatest number, and the wisest, accept none of
this but believe in a single divinity, unknown, eternal, infinite,
inexplicable, diffused throughout the universe not materially
but by his power in a manner that is beyond human understanding. They address him as their parent. To him they attribute
the origin, growth, progress, development and end of all things,
and they reserve divine honours to him alone.

In fact, all the other creeds, in spite of their differences, agree
with this last group that there is one supreme being, the creator
and governor of the universe, and together they call him Mithras in their native speech.[49] But they diverge in their perception
of the same being, each believing that whatever they hold as
highest can be identified with that one unique nature to whose
majesty and divine power is attributed, by the consensus of all

nations, sovereignty over all things. Gradually, however, they are all dispensing with superstitions of this sort and are uniting in a common religion that seems to surpass the others in its reasonableness. And there's no doubt that these other beliefs would have vanished long ago but for the fact that any mishap which struck someone deliberating a change of faith was seen not as an accident but, thanks to superstitious fear, as some divine intervention – as if the deity whose cult was being abandoned were avenging an insult.

But when they had heard from us the name of Christ, his teachings, his life, his miracles, and the no less wonderful constancy of the many martyrs who, by the voluntary shedding of their blood, have attracted to their faith so many different nations, you'd scarcely believe the strength of feeling with which they embraced it too, either through the secret prompting of God, or because it resembles that school of thought which is most widely accepted among them. Mind you, I suspect that a major factor here was their discovery that Christ approved the communal life of his disciples, and that it's still practised by the most authentic Christian communities.[50] Whatever the cause, no small number of them embraced our religion and were purified in the holy water of baptism. To my regret there was no priest among the four of us who survived (for fate had claimed two of our companions), so that although the converts had been admitted to the other sacraments, they still lacked those which among us can only be conferred by priests. Nonetheless, they know well what these are and have an intense desire to receive them. In fact, they debate earnestly among themselves as to whether someone chosen from their own number might receive holy orders without the agency of a Christian bishop.[51] It seemed that they were about to select such a person but they hadn't yet done so by the time I left.

Those who haven't adopted Christianity make no attempt to put others off, nor do they clash with those who are converted. There was an occasion while I was there when one member of our community was arrested: as soon as he was baptised, and against our advice, he began to speak publicly about the Christian faith with more enthusiasm than good sense. He

became so carried away that he not only placed our faith above
all others but noisily condemned the rest as profane and their
followers as impious, sacrilegious and destined to eternal fire.
After he had preached like this for quite some time they seized
him and tried him on a charge not of religious contempt but of
creating public disorder, and he was duly convicted and sentenced to exile. For it is one of their most ancient tenets that no
one should suffer harm for his religion.[52]

Utopus saw that prior to his arrival the inhabitants had been
constantly quarrelling over religious issues, and he fully recognized that because the sects were generally in disagreement and
fought for their country as separate groups, this had presented
him with a perfect opportunity to conquer them all. Thus, at
the very outset, having gained the victory, he decreed that everyone should be free to follow the religion of his choice, and
might even endeavour to convert others to it – so long as the
arguments were presented with calm and restraint; but if persuasion failed to convince, then the advocate shouldn't rail at
other faiths or use violence or insulting language. The penalty
for such fanaticism would be exile or servitude.

Utopus laid down these rules not just for the sake of peace,
which he could see was being radically threatened by endless
strife and irreconcilable hatreds, but also because he thought
that such a policy would work in the interests of religion itself.
In these matters he was in no hurry to dogmatize, as if unsure
whether God desires to be worshipped in various ways and
hence inspires different people with different ideas. Certainly,
he judged it arrogant folly to impose what you believe to be
true on others using threats and violence. He was far-sighted
enough to sense that if one religion was evidently true and all
others false, then – provided that things are handled with reason
and moderation – the truth would sooner or later emerge and
assert itself by its own inner strength. But if the issue is settled
with weapons and uproar, seeing that the worst men are always
the most inflexible, then the purest and most holy religion will
be choked by empty superstitions, just like corn sown among
thistles and scrub. Consequently, Utopus left matters open,
making each person free to follow his own beliefs, except that

he solemnly and strictly forbade anyone to fall so far beneath
the dignity of human nature as to think that the soul dies with
the body or that the universe is governed by chance rather than
by providence.

Accordingly the Utopians hold that after this life punishments are decreed for vices and rewards granted for virtue.
Anyone who denies this they regard as a renegade to humanity,
since he's reduced the aspiring nature of his own soul to the
level of an animal carcass. Even less will they admit him as a
citizen since, unless he's checked by fear, he'll have no regard
for their laws or customs. It's obvious that anyone who has no
fear beyond the law, and has no hope beyond this life, will do
all he can either to evade his country's laws by cunning or to
thrust them aside by force, so as to gratify his selfish interests.
For this reason no one holding such views is accorded honours,
entrusted with official functions or given public responsibility;
he's universally looked down on as inert and sluggish. No punishment is imposed on him because they don't consider that it's
within the power of man to believe whatever he wants; equally,
they don't use threats to make him disguise his beliefs, nor will
they allow any prevarication or lying, which they consider
every bit as bad as open contempt for the law. It's true that they
ban him from airing his convictions, especially among the general mass of the people; but otherwise, in the presence of the
priests and other men of the wiser sort, they not only allow it
but actually encourage it, confident that in the long run his
aberration will yield to reason.

There are others, and no small number at that, who aren't
subject to the same restraints since their position isn't wholly
irrational or depraved: these go to the other extreme, suppos-
ing that brute creatures have immortal souls, though not
comparable to ours in dignity nor destined to equal happiness.
Nearly all Utopians are utterly convinced that human happiness after death will be beyond measure, and so while they feel
sorrow for those who are sick they don't extend this to anyone
who dies, unless he was snatched from life reluctantly and in
distress. For they regard such conduct as an ominous sign, as
though the soul, burdened with guilt and despair, feared death

through some inner sense of punishment to come. They also think that God is hardly likely to be pleased by the arrival of a person who, when summoned, doesn't come willingly but is dragged off resisting. When they witness a death of this kind they are shocked and transport the corpse in melancholy silence; after praying that God will be favourable to the soul of the deceased and overlook his weaknesses, they cover it with earth. In contrast, when someone embraces death and dies full of hope they don't mourn him but carry out the last rites with singing, commending his soul to God with deep affection. Finally, with reverence rather than sorrow, they cremate him, then erect a column on the spot, on which his achievements are recorded. When they've returned to their homes they talk about the kind of person he was and about what he did, and no part of his life is more frequently or gladly referred to than his joyful death.

In their view such a celebration of a life well lived is both a powerful incitement to virtue for those who survive and a fitting form of reverence for the dead, whom they also believe to be present as they are spoken of, although invisible to the dullness of human sight. For it wouldn't be in keeping with their state of felicity if the dead lacked freedom to go where they wanted, and it would be ungrateful on their part if they were to drop all desire to see those friends to whom they had been bound by mutual love and by charity when alive. The Utopians assume that charity, like the other virtues in good men, will be increased after death rather than diminished. They believe, therefore, that the dead move among the living, observing their sayings and their actions, and so they tackle their enterprises with all the more confidence because of their trust in such protectors. This belief in the presence of their ancestors inhibits them from any secret acts of dishonesty.[53]

As for fortune-telling and other such empty and superstitious forms of prediction, highly rated among other nations, the Utopians have no time for them and laugh at them. But miracles that occur without any natural cause they venerate as evidence of God's active presence; they claim that such events occur frequently among them, and sometimes in the context of a major crisis they confidently offer up public prayers for one, and obtain it.

They consider that contemplation of nature and the prayerful adoration that it inspires are a form of worship pleasing to God. But there are some, and these by no means few, who on religious grounds disregard literature and take no interest in study, and yet have no leisure. They are resolved to gain happiness after death solely by good work and the service of others. So some look after the sick; others remake roads, dredge ditches, repair bridges, dig turf, sand and stones; yet others fell trees and cut them up, or convey wood, grain and other essentials to the cities by wagon. Their services extend to private employers as well as the public, and they work harder than slaves. Whatever work is so rough, exhausting and filthy that most people would be put off by the sweat, disgust and tedium involved, they carry out willingly and even happily. Through their continual toil and labour they generate leisure for other people, and yet they claim no credit for this: they don't complain about the lifestyle of others or elevate their own. The more they put themselves in the position of slaves the more they're held in honour by everyone.

There are two sects among them. One of celibates, who refrain not just from all sexual activity but also from eating meat (and some from any animal products whatsoever); they wholly reject all the pleasures of this present life as harmful, and feel a great longing for those of the life to come, which they express through their exertions and by night-long vigils. In the meantime, buoyed up by the hope of entering it soon, they are lively and good-spirited. Members of the other sect are just as keen on work but opt for marriage: they don't reject the solace it offers, and consider that they owe the act itself to nature and offspring to their homeland. They don't refuse any pleasure as long as it doesn't interfere with their work. They enjoy eating animal flesh because they believe that by it they will be better fitted for every kind of work. The Utopians regard this sect as more sensible, but the other one as holier. Were the latter to justify their preference for celibacy over marriage and for a harsh life over one of ease on purely rational grounds, everyone would laugh at them. As it is, since they admit to being driven by religious motives, the Utopians look up to them and hold them in reverence – for they are extremely careful to avoid any overhasty judgements where religion is concerned. These, then, are the kind of men that in their language they call Buthrescas, a name that can be translated as 'religiosi' in Latin, that is, 'god-fearing'.[54]

Utopian priests are of exceptional holiness, and consequently very few in number. There are no more than thirteen in each city, one for each temple, except in time of war; then seven of them go with the army, and in their absence they are replaced by substitutes. Once the original priests return the substitutes revert to their former status; in the meanwhile, until by due succession they replace the priests who die, they act as assistants to the chief priest (for one is placed over all the others). They are elected by the people in the same manner as other officials, by secret ballot to avoid faction, and those chosen are ordained by their fellow priests. They preside over religious ceremonies, oversee religious affairs and act as guardians of public morals; to be summoned by them and rebuked for unacceptable conduct is regarded as deeply shameful. As it is their duty to exhort and to forewarn, so the restraint and punishment of criminals is the responsibility of the governor and other magistrates; but the priests do exclude from their sacred rites those whom they know to be incorrigible offenders. Scarcely any other punishment is more dreaded than this, for those affected endure public ignomy and are tormented by inner fears of divine retribution. Even their physical security is unsure, for unless they can swiftly persuade the priests of their repentance, they will be seized and punished by the senate for their impiety.

The education of children and young people is the responsibility of the priests, and it's no less concerned with morality and virtue than with the study of good literature. For they take the greatest care from the outset to instil in the pupils' minds – while they are still eager and impressionable – principles that benefit the life of the community. Whatever is lodged in the minds of the young accompanies them as adults through the course of their lives and can be of great value in preserving the state of the commonwealth, which only succumbs to those vices that arise from perverse attitudes. The wives of the priests are the most highly esteemed in the country – unless, of course, the priests happen to be women, for their sex is not excluded. But it's unusual, and then only a widow of mature years is chosen.

No officials are held in greater honour among the Utopians, even to the extent that if priests do commit a crime, they aren't exposed to public judgment but are left alone to God and their consciences. For it is regarded as unfitting to lay mortal hands on someone, however guilty, who has been specially consecrated to God like some holy offering. This practice is easier for them since their priests are few and are selected with the greatest care. For it's quite against the grain that a man chosen as best among the good, and raised to such eminence solely on account of his virtues, will slide down into corruption and vice. And even if such a thing should occur, given the instability of human nature, there would be no need to fear serious consequences in the public sphere since priests are so few in number and have no specific power apart from their moral influence. Indeed, they have such a small number of priests in case the dignity of the order, at present held in such high regard, might be debased by extending it too broadly.[55] They think that it would be difficult, in particular, to find many candidates adequate to such an elevated office, which calls for a more than ordinary degree of virtue.

The esteem in which their priests are held is scarcely greater among them than among foreign nations, and it's easy enough, I think, to see how this arises. For when their forces are engaged in battle, the Utopian priests, clothed in their sacred garments, place themselves a little apart and, kneeling and with their hands raised to heaven, they pray in the first place for peace, and next for the success of their own troops – but with the minimum of bloodshed on either side.[56] If victory is theirs, then they run into the line of battle and check the ferocity of their own soldiers against the vanquished. Just to have seen and called out to one of them is enough to save your life, and to touch their flowing robes protects your possessions against the hazards of war. This conduct has brought them such respect among all nations, and such genuine authority, that they have saved their own citizens from the enemy no less often than they have preserved the enemy from their own troops. Indeed, it has sometimes happened that when the Utopians' own line had been broken and their desperate forces were turning in flight, even as the enemy rushed in to kill and pillage, the intervention of the priests put a halt to the carnage and, once the armies were separated, just conditions for peace were drawn up and agreed. For there's never been a people anywhere that's so savage, cruel and barbarous as not to regard the priests' persons as sacred and inviolable.

The Utopians observe as feast days the first and last days of each month, and also of the year; the latter they divide into months which are indicated by the orbit of the moon, just as the revolution of the sun defines the year. The first days they call Cynemerni in their language, and the last days Trapemerni, meaning 'First-feasts' and 'Last-feasts'. Their temples are impressive not only on account of the manner of their construction but also because of their capacity to hold large crowds – an essential feature since there are so few of them. Yet they are dimly lit, and not from some architectural oversight but on the advice of the priests, who think that too much light scatters attention whereas a dim and uncertain light focuses the mind and stirs religious feelings.

While religion there isn't identical for everyone, yet all its forms, however varied and numerous they may be, come together in veneration of the divine nature, like different paths running to a common destination, and for that reason nothing is seen or heard in their temples that doesn't fit in with what they all hold in common. Should a sect have some religious practice that is peculiar to it alone, then that is performed within the confines of a private house; the public rites are conducted according to rubrics which in no way detract from the private observances. Consequently, no images of the gods are to be found in their temples so that everyone is left free to form a personal image of God in keeping with his belief. They don't invoke God by any specific name apart from that of Mithras, a designation that they all agree in applying to the unique nature of divine majesty, however that may be defined, and no prayers are adopted that can't be said by everyone without offence to their particular sect.

So on the evening of the Last-feast they gather together in the temples, and while still fasting give thanks to God for their prosperity in the month or year that's about to end. Then, on the morning of the next day, or First-feast, they all converge on the temples and pray together that the month or year just beginning will prove a time of prosperity and happiness. But on that day of First-feast, before they leave home for the temple, wives kneel before their husbands and children before their parents in order to confess their faults, whether in their actions or through neglect of their duties, and to ask forgiveness for these lapses. In this way any small cloud of resentment that hangs over the household is dispelled, and they can attend the sacrifices with minds that are pure and at peace; it's regarded as sacrilege to participate with a burdened conscience. Those conscious of hatred or anger towards another person won't take part in the sacrifices until they've been reconciled with them and have subdued their own passions, fearful of some swift and terrible punishment.

When they come to the temple, the men draw to the right-hand side and the women to the left, and they then arrange themselves so that males are seated in front of the father of their particular family, while the mother of the family oversees the ranks of its female members. This ensures that everyone's every action is observed in public by those very people under whose authority and control they are governed at home. They take particular care that the young are placed alongside their elders, just in case children left to themselves might fritter away in silly distractions the time they ought to spend in learning religious awe of the gods, the greatest and almost the only incentive to virtue.

They don't slaughter any animals in their sacrifices since they can't believe that a merciful God, who gave life to all living creatures so that they might live, is going to take delight in bloodshed or killing. They burn incense and other fragrant things of that kind, and in addition they offer great numbers of candles. It's not that they're unaware that such practices don't actually benefit the divine nature, any more than human prayers might, but they find this harmless manner of worship pleasing. And they feel that through these fragrant odours, lights and ceremonies the worshippers are moved – in some inexplicable way – and raise themselves with greater liveliness of spirit to the worship of God.

In the temple the congregation wears white garments. The priest is clothed in varicoloured vestments remarkable for their embroidery and design, though the materials are not particularly opulent: there is no gold woven into the cloth or any precious stones attached. Instead the garments are made out of the plumage of different birds with such skill and craftsmanship that the costliest fabric couldn't match their value.[57] Further, it's said that the birds' feathers and the specific patterns in which they are displayed on the priest's robes convey certain esoteric mysteries which, when properly interpreted (and the priests are careful to hand on the meaning), remind the worshippers of the benefits they have received from God, and of the duty they owe him in return, as well as to each other.

When the priest, dressed in these vestments, first emerges from the sacristy, all those present prostrate themselves in reverence; such a profound stillness pervades the building that the scene inspires a sense of awe, as if the congregation were in the presence of a divinity. After remaining for a while on the ground, they rise at a signal from the priest and sing God's praises to the accompaniment of musical instruments, most of which are quite different in appearance from those seen in our part of the world. Many of them surpass those we have in the sweetness of their sounds, but others are not really comparable. Yet there is one respect in which the Utopians are certainly well ahead of us, and that's the manner in which all their music, whether it's played on instruments or sung, imitates and expresses natural feelings, and so matches the sound to meaning that whether the prayer is one of entreaty or joy, calm or perplexity, sorrow or anger, the form of the melody embodies the mood in such a way that it penetrates the minds of the hearers, possessing them and stirring their deepest emotions. To conclude the ceremony, the priest and the people say together certain prescribed prayers which are so worded that whatever they recite in common everyone can apply inwardly to himself.

In these prayers each worshipper acknowledges God as creator and lord of the universe and the source of all goodness, giving thanks for all the blessings he's received, and in particular that God's favour has placed him in the happiest commonwealth conceivable and in that religion which he hopes to be the truest. But in case he should be mistaken about this, and there is some form of government or religion better and more pleasing to God, he then prays that God will allow him to discover it, for he's ready to follow wherever he may lead him. If, however, this commonwealth is the best and their religion is the truest, then he prays that he will both confirm him in it and attract the rest of humanity to a similar manner of life and the same understanding of God – unless, that is, there's something in the existing variety of religions that meets his hidden purpose.

Next, he prays that after an easy death God will take him to himself, though whether sooner or later he doesn't dare to ask. Nevertheless, should it be acceptable to God's majesty, he would much rather go to him at the cost of a most painful death than be kept from him for a longer time, however flourishing his course of life may be. Once this prayer has been said, they prostrate themselves once more, and after a pause they rise and disperse to lunch, passing the remainder of the day in games and military exercises.

Now I've described to you as truthfully as I can the likeness of that commonwealth which, without any hesitation, I hold to be not just the best but the only one that can rightfully lay claim to that title. Elsewhere people are always talking about the commonwealth, but they are really concerned about their private interests; here, where nothing is private, public issues are taken seriously. And both attitudes are right, for elsewhere there can't be many who fail to see that unless a man looks after his own interests he'll die of hunger, however prosperous the commonwealth may be. Necessity drives him to consider his own requirements rather than those of the public, that's to say, of other people. By contrast here, where all things are common to everyone,[58] provided that the public warehouses remain full, nobody needs fear that he'll be short of anything for his own use. Indeed, the distribution of resources is anything but stingy: there no one is poor or reduced to begging, and while nobody possesses anything everyone is rich.

For what greater riches can a man hope for than to live free from care and with a joyful, tranquil mind, not worried about supporting himself or being harassed by his wife's endless demands, nor apprehensive about his son's poverty or anxious about his daughter's dowry? Instead he's assured of subsistence and happiness for himself and all his dependants – wife, sons, grandsons, great-grandsons, great-great-grandsons, and that whole panoply of descendants that aristocrats like to picture to themselves. What's more, those who worked once but are now too weak to do so are no less cared for than those who are still at work.

At this point I'd like to see someone compare this Utopian equity with the justice of other nations, among whom I'll be hanged if I can detect the slightest trace of either. For what sort of justice is it when some aristocrat, goldsmith, moneylender or, for that matter, any such individual who either does nothing at all or else something quite remote from the real needs of the commonwealth, enjoys a life of luxury and elegance thanks to his idleness or his inessential services, while at the same time a labourer, a wagoner, an artisan or a farm-worker sweats so hard and so long that a beast of burden could scarcely bear it, and at work so essential that no commonwealth could survive for a year without it; yet they earn such pathetic recompense and live such wretched lives that the condition of beasts actually seems preferable, since beasts don't have to toil without a break and their food is scarcely worse – in fact, to them it's more tasty – nor do they fret about the future. But men like these are compelled for the present to labour that brings scant reward, and are haunted by the prospect of a penniless old age, for their daily wage is so far from meeting their current needs that there's no chance of any surplus being put aside that they might rely on when they're old.

Now isn't it an inequitable and selfish society where such rewards are lavished on the nobility (as they're called), and on goldsmiths and others of that sort, who are either parasites, or flatterers, or purveyors of idle pleasures? And where, by contrast, no decent provision is made for farm-workers, or colliers, or labourers, or carters or artisans, without whom the commonwealth couldn't even function? When their best years have been used up in drudgery, when they are worn down by age and sickness and are quite destitute, an ungrateful society, disregarding their long hours of work and the extent of their services, repays them with a wretched death. But there's more: the rich are forever fleecing the poor of some of their daily pittance, not only by private fraud but even by official legislation. In this way what initially seemed an injustice, namely that those who deserved most from the commonwealth received least, has now been converted from an abuse into an act of justice by the passing of a law. So when I survey and assess all the different political systems flourishing today, nothing else presents itself – God help me – but a conspiracy of the rich, who look after their own interests under the name and title of the commonwealth.[59] They plot and contrive schemes and devices by which, for a start, they can cling on to whatever they have already accumulated by shady means without any fear of losing it, and then take advantage of the poor by acquiring their works and their labour at the lowest possible cost. Once the rich, in the name of the community (and that, of course, includes the poor), have decreed that these fraudulent practices are to be observed, they become laws.

Yet when these vile men, with their boundless greed, have shared out among themselves those resources which might have provided for everyone's needs, they're still far from achieving the happiness of the Utopian commonwealth. There, once the use of money had been abolished and avarice along with it, what a mass of troubles was cut away, what a harvest of crimes uprooted! For who can fail to see that fraud, theft, pillaging, disputes, riots, strife, rebellion, murder, treason, poisoning, all those crimes that repeated punishment fails to deter, would die out with the abolition of money. And at the very moment when money vanished, so too would fear, anxiety, grief, stress and wakeful nights; even poverty itself, which seems to be just the lack of money, would instantly vanish if money was completely suppressed.

To clarify the point, just picture in your mind some barren and unproductive season in which many thousands of people died from hunger: now I'll wager that if at the end of that famine the storehouses of the rich were searched, sufficient grain would be found that if it had been distributed among those struck down by starvation or pestilence, no one would even have noticed the shortcomings of soil or weather. The necessities of life might so easily have been provided, except that hallowed money – which was manifestly devised to give access to such essentials – alone blocks our path to them. I'm confident that even the rich feel this, nor are they unaware that it's better to lack nothing we really require than to wallow in an excess of superfluous things, to be preserved from a multitude of evils rather than hemmed in by great wealth. Indeed, I've not a shred of doubt that either the claims of self-interest or the authority of Christ our saviour (who in the extent of his wisdom could scarcely fail to know what is best and in his goodness to advocate it) would easily have drawn the whole world to adopt the laws of this commonwealth, but for the resistance of one great monster, pride, the prince and begetter of all plagues.

Pride measures prosperity not by her own good fortune but rather by the ill-fortune of others. She wouldn't even want to be a goddess unless some wretches remained whom she could taunt and push around, by whose misfortunes her own happiness would shine more brightly and whose poverty she might vex and provoke by flaunting her wealth.[60] This serpent from hell infiltrates human hearts and, like a sucker-fish, holds them back and hinders them from embracing a better way of life. Seeing that pride is too deeply embedded in human nature to be easily torn out, I rejoice that this form of a commonwealth – which I could happily wish for everyone – has at least been attained by the Utopians; by the way of life they have adopted they have laid the foundations for a commonwealth that is not only the happiest but even, in so far as human foresight can judge these things, likely to last for ever. Since on the domestic front they've uprooted ambition and faction, along with the other vices, there's no danger of internal strife, which has so often been responsible for sapping the strength of many well-fortified cities. Just so long as social harmony and sound institutions survive at home, the envy of all neighbouring princes, who have often tried in vain, won't be able to threaten or shake their sovereignty.

When Raphael had finished his account, I was left with the sense that not a few of the practices which arose from Utopian laws and customs were patently absurd – not only their manner of waging war, their religious beliefs and observances, and other such matters, but above all else that which is the linchpin of their entire social order, their life in common without any use of money. This one thing by itself utterly subverts all nobility, magnificence, splendour and majesty, which according to popular opinion are the proper ornaments and honours of the commonwealth.[61] However, I knew that he was weary from talking, and it wasn't at all clear to me whether he would tolerate a contrary view, especially when I recalled that he had rebuked certain individuals who feared that they wouldn't pass for wise unless they found something to niggle about in the proposals of others, and so for that reason, having praised their way of life and his exposition, I took him by the hand and led him in to dinner, but not before I had said that we would have another opportunity to probe into these matters and to discuss them more extensively. If only this might happen one day!

Meanwhile, although I can hardly agree with all that was said, even by a man who is without question both erudite and experienced in human affairs, yet I freely admit that there are many features in that Utopian commonwealth which I might more truly wish for than expect to see in our own cities.

Appendix 1
'Between friends all is common'

This is the opening adage from the 1515 edition of Erasmus' *Adages*,[1] in which he surveys the ideas of the ancient world about community and ownership.

Between friends all is common. Since there is nothing more wholesome or more generally accepted than this proverb, it seemed good to place it at the head of this collection of adages. If only it were so fixed in men's minds as it is frequent on everybody's lips, most of the evils of our lives would promptly be removed. From this proverb Socrates deduced that all things belong to all good men, just as they do to the gods. For to the gods, said he, belong all things; good men are friends of the gods; and among friends all possessions are in common. Therefore good men own everything. It is quoted by Euripides in his *Orestes*: 'Shared in common are the possessions of friends', and again in the *Phoenissae*: 'All grief of friends is shared.' Again in the *Andromache*: 'True friends have nothing of their own, but with them all is common.' Terence says in the *Adelphoe*: 'For there is an old proverb, that between friends all is common.' It is said that this was also in Menander, in a play of the same name. Cicero in the first book of the *De officiis* says, 'As the Greek proverb has it, all things are in common between friends', and it is quoted by Aristotle in the eighth book of his *Ethics* and by Plato in the *Laws*, book 5. Plato is trying to show that the happiest condition of a society consists in the community of all possessions: 'So the first kind of city and polity and the best laws are found where the old saying is maintained as much as possible throughout the whole city; and the saying is that friends really have all things in common.' Plato also says that a state would be happy and blessed in which these words 'mine' and 'not mine' were never to be heard. But it is extraordinary how Christians dislike this common ownership of Plato's, how in fact they cast stones at it, although nothing was ever said by a pagan philosopher which comes closer to the mind of Christ. Aristotle in book 2 of the *Politics* moderates the opinion of Plato by saying that possessions and legal ownership should be vested in certain definite persons, but otherwise all should be in common according to the proverb, for the sake of convenience, virtuous living and social harmony. Martial in book 2 pokes fun at a certain Candidus who was always quoting this adage, but otherwise gave nothing to his friends: 'O Candidus, what's mine is yours, you say; / Grandly you chant this maxim night and day', and the epigram ends thus: '"What's mine is yours", yet naught you give away.'[2] An elegant remark of Theophrastus is quoted in Plutarch, in the little essay entitled 'On Brotherly Love': 'If friends' possessions are in common, then friends' friends still more should be in common too.'[3] Cicero in the first book of the *De legibus* seems to attribute this adage to Pythagoras, when he says: 'Hence that word of Pythagoras "Between friends things are in common, and friendship is equality."' In Diogenes Laertius also Timaeus reports that this saying first began with Pythagoras.[4] Aulus Gellius in his *Attic Nights*, book 1 chapter 9, bears witness that not only was Pythagoras the author of this saying, but that he also instituted a kind of sharing of life and property in this way, the very thing that Christ wants to happen among Christians. For all those who were admitted by Pythagoras into that well-known band who followed his instruction would give to the common fund whatever money and family property they possessed. This is called in Latin, in a word which expresses the facts, *coenobium*,[5] clearly from community of life and fortunes.

NOTES

1. Translated by Margaret Mann Phillips in *Collected Works of Erasmus* (University of Toronto Press, 1974–), 31, 29–30.
2. Martial, *Epigrams* 2:43, 1–2 and 16.
3. Plutarch, *Moralia* 490e.
4. Diogenes Laertius, *Lives of the Philosophers* 8.10.
5. In Christian use the word comes to mean a monastic community.

Appendix 2
An Account of the
Taíno People

The following text is taken from the *First Decade of the Ocean* by Peter Martyr d'Anghiera (*On the New World*, 1511),[1] in which he relates the voyages of Columbus. Here he describes the elevated moral ideas of the Taíno people and compares their way of life to the classical myth of a Golden Age as depicted by Ovid in his *Metamorphoses*.

While the admiral was listening to divine service on the shore, they noticed one of their chief men; he was an octogenarian and an important man, but for all that naked, with many in attendance on him. He stood by in wonder, his eyes and face intent, while the service was being carried out; then he presented the admiral with the gift of a basket, which he was carrying in his hand, full of his country's fruits, and sitting in his presence, with Diego Colón as interpreter, who understood their language since they had come nearer home, he made a speech as follows: 'News has been brought us that trusting in your powerful hand you have voyaged by these lands until now unknown to you, and have brought no ordinary fear to the people living there; I warn you them to be aware that souls have two paths when they leap forth from the body, one gloomy and hideous, prepared for those who cause trouble and are the enemies of the human race, the other delightful and pleasant, appointed for those who in their lives have loved peace and quiet among nations. If therefore you remember that you are mortal and that rewards will be duly assigned to each in accordance with his present actions, you will attack no one.'

These and several other remarks were translated by the interpreter from the islands for the commander, who was amazed at a judgement like that coming from a naked man; he replied that he was thoroughly informed on all the things he had said about the different journeys and rewards of souls on leaving the body, indeed he had even thought up to this point that they were unknown to the old man and the other inhabitants of these parts, living as they did content with nature. But as for the rest he replied that he had been sent by the king and queen of the Spains to pacify all those shores of the world which had been unknown to this moment, that is to make war on the cannibals and any other natives who were wicked men, subdue them and apply the punishments they deserved, but to protect and honour the guiltless because of their virtues; therefore neither he nor anyone else who was not disposed to do harm should fear him. Far from it; they should disclose any injustice which might have been visited on them, or on other good men, by their neighbours.

The commander's words pleased the old man so much that he declared he would very gladly go with the commander, though he was now growing weary with age, and this would have been done, if his wife and his sons had not blocked him. Yet he was utterly amazed that the admiral was subject to another man's command, but when he heard an account, through the interpreter, of the magnificence and size of their majesties' ceremonies, their power, their adornments and their equipment for war, the size of their cities and the splendour of their towns, he was even more dumbstruck. Rather sadly then, his wife and son prostrate before his feet with tears in their eyes, this distinguished old man remained fast, asking again and again whether the sky was the land which produced great men of this character.

It has been discovered that with them the earth, like the sun and water, is common, nor do 'mine and yours', the seeds of all evils, fall among them. For they are content with so little that in that vast earth there is an excess of land to farm rather than a lack of anything. Theirs is a golden age: they do not hedge their estates with ditches, walls or hedges; they live with open gardens; without laws, without books, without judges, of their own nature, they cultivate what is right. They judge he is evil and wicked who takes pleasure in inflicting injury on anyone. Nonetheless they cultivate maize, yucca and *ajes*,[2] as we have said happens in Hispaniola.

NOTES

1. From Geoffrey Eatough, ed. and trans., *Selections from Peter Martyr*, Repertorium Columbianum, vol. 5 (Turnhout: Brepols, 1998), pp. 68–9.
2. Tuberous roots, which had a flavour of chestnuts when cooked.

Glossary of Names

Abraxa: the ancient name for Utopia; it may be derived from the Gnostic theologian Basilides (2nd century AD), who applied it to the highest of 365 heavens, but the main point here is that it sounds exotic.

Achorians: 'people without a country', from Greek *a-choros*, 'without a place'.

Ademus: 'people-less', from Greek *a-demos*, 'without a people', the current name for the governor of a Utopian city; see also Barzanes.

Alaopolitans: 'citizens without a people', from Greek *a-laos-polites*.

Amaurot: 'spectral city', from Greek *amauros*, 'dim' or 'shadowy'.

Anemolians: 'blown up, boastful', from Greek *anemolios*, 'windy'.

Anemolius: as with the Anemolians, but here applied to the poet.

Anyder: 'waterless', from Greek *a-nydros*, 'without water'.

Barzanes: 'son of Zeus', the ancient name for the governor of a Utopian city, from the Hebrew *bar-*, 'son of', and *Zanos*, the Greek Doric form for 'of Zeus'; More would have encountered the name Mithrobarzanes in Lucian's *Menippus*, which he had translated.

Buthrescas: 'extra religious', from Greek *bou* (huge) and *threskos* (religious); the word is probably meant to match (not without irony) the term 'religious' as used in the Church to refer to professed members of orders such as the Franciscans or Benedictines.

Hythloday: 'purveyor (or distributor) of nonsense', from Greek *hythlos* (nonsense) and *hodao* (to trade in, sell) or, possibly, *daiein* (to distribute); his first name Raphael evokes the archangel who guided Tobias (Tobit 5:4) and can mean heavenly physician or healer.

Macarians: 'happy people', from Greek *makarios* (happy).

Nephelogetes: 'cloud-born', from Greek *nephele* (cloud) and *genetes* (begotten).

phylarch: 'ruler of a tribe', from Greek *phylarchos*; the current name for a syphogrant (see below).

polylerites: 'people of much nonsense', from Greek *polus* (much) and *leros* (nonsense).

syphogrant: the ancient name for a phylarch; possibly from Greek *sophos* (wise) and *gerontes* (old men), but less flattering alternatives have been suggested. He represents thirty households.

tranibor: the ancient name for a proto- or chief phylarch who oversees ten syphograncies; the basis is obscure, but may come from Greek *tranos* (plain, clear) and *boros* (gluttonous), giving something like 'plain-eater'.

Tricius Apinatus: 'stuff and nonsense', derived from a Latin proverb which occurs in Erasmus' *Adages* (*CWE* 31, 184).

Utopia: 'no-place', from Greek *ou-* (not) and *topos* (place); it is a Greek rendering of More's original Latin title *Nusquama*, 'nowhere' or 'no place'.

Zapoletes: 'busy sellers', from Greek *poletes* (seller) and the intensive *za-*, a reference to the commercial acumen of Swiss mercenaries.

Notes

Abbreviations

Utopia marks an important point in Thomas More's intellectual association with Erasmus, and we now have the advantage of two major editions of their works. I have used the following abbreviations to refer to them:

CWE: *Collected Works of Erasmus* (Toronto University Press, 1974–).
CWM: *The Complete Works of St. Thomas More* (Yale University Press, 1963–97).

Anemolius' Stanza on the Island of Utopia

1. *by Anemolius*: Probably by More himself, the stanza may be a hit at John Skelton (1460?–1529), 'laureate poet' at Oxford and Cambridge, who did not share More's Greek interests; for Anemolius see the Glossary of Names.
2. *Plato's state*: In his *Republic*, Plato (*c.* 429–347 BC) composed the seminal work of Western political thought and *Utopia* is closely engaged with it; the point here is that Plato's theoretical account is trounced by More's fictional 'demonstration'.
3. *'Happy-place'*: *Eutopia*, a pun derived from the Greek prefix *eu-*, 'happy, fortunate', and *topos*, 'place'.

Thomas More's First Letter to Peter Giles

1. *Peter Giles*: Peter Giles or Gillis (1486–1533) was a humanist and friend of Erasmus (1469?–1536). Combining literary studies with legal and administrative duties in a similar manner to More

himself, he became Clerk to the city of Antwerp in 1512; in 1517 he and Erasmus sent More a diptych of their portraits by the Flemish artist Quentin Metsys. As his letter to Jerome Busleyden makes clear, he played an active part in preparing the final text of *Utopia*.

2. *leaves just nothing . . . writing*: In January 1517 More apologizes to Erasmus: 'But you will forgive me, my dearest Erasmus, for I am under such a constant pressure of business, I have neither time to write nor energy to think' (Letter 513, *CWE* 4, 183).

3. *John Clement . . . harvest*: John Clement (d. 1572) studied at St Paul's School before becoming More's servant-pupil; later he taught Greek at Oxford before entering on a distinguished career as a physician; he died as a Catholic exile in the Netherlands.

4. *honest rather than clever*: The distinction is between telling an untruth in good faith and deliberately misleading with a lie; here as elsewhere More is playing with the issue of fiction and its 'truth'.

5. *snub-nosed . . . dreads water*: The nose expresses derision or contempt (as in Horace, *Satires* 1.6.5 and 2.8.64), so to be snub-nosed is to lack a sense of irony. Dread of water is a symptom of rabies.

6. *'out of range' . . . not a hair left to grab them by*: 'Out of range' is included by Erasmus in his *Adages* I.iii.93 (*CWE* 31, 311). The bald-headed critics are presumably tonsured clerics like those Franciscans who, as More warns Erasmus, have 'taken an oath that they will read right through [your works] with the greatest care, and not understand anything' (Letter 481, *CWE* 4, 115).

7. *it's too late to be wise*: Another Erasmian adage, I.i.28, *CWE* 31, 76–7.

Peter Giles's Letter to Jerome Busleyden

1. *Jerome Busleyden*: Jerome Busleyden (c. 1470–1517) was a prominent statesman and patron of learning who also contributed a letter to the first edition of *Utopia*; during the summer of 1515 More visited his house in Mechelen, and wrote Latin verses on his collection of Roman coins.

2. *Ulysses . . . Vespucci seems to have seen nothing*: The fame of Ulysses (Odysseus) as a traveller came from Homer's account of his spectacular adventures in the *Odyssey*; to include in the comparison Amerigo Vespucci (1454–1512), with whom Raphael sails to the New World, suggests that Giles, like More, knew

that at least some of his claimed travels were a hoax. See Book One, note 6.

3. *I am so caught up ... Utopia*: Giles is playing with the rhetorical figure of *vividness* (Greek: *enargeia*), which aims to transport the reader to the scene described, like imaginary travel.

4. *little notes in the margin*: The marginal notes are not printed in this translation, but the more significant ones are referred to in these endnotes.

5. *Maecenas*: Roman statesman (*c.* 70–8 BC), proverbial for his patronage of poets, including Horace (65–8 BC) and Virgil (70–19 BC).

Thomas More's Second Letter to Peter Giles

1. *Thomas More sends . . . Giles*: This letter only appears in the second edition (Paris, 1517), but it continues the Lucianic game about fiction and history that More is playing with Giles

2. *their office*: The office is the sequence of prayers, or 'hours', that the clergy are obliged to recite daily.

3. *outlandish names ... signify nothing*: Which is just what they do signify: see the Glossary of Names.

4. *By Pollux! . . . at his birth*: Terence (*fl. c.* 160 BC), *Andria* (*The Woman of Andros*) IV.iv.770–71.

BOOK ONE

1. *matters . . . far from trifling*: These matters concerned the important commercial traffic between England and the Netherlands, notably in wool, which was in serious danger as Prince Charles (1500–1558), later Emperor Charles V, sought a French alliance.

2. *Cuthbert Tunstall*: A close friend of More and of Erasmus and a gifted diplomat, Cuthbert Tunstall (1474–1559) became Master of the Rolls, a senior legal appointment within the Court of Chancery, in May 1516. Later he was in succession Bishop of London (1523–9) and of Durham (1530–59).

3. *to show the sun with a lantern*: The proverb 'To hold a candle to the sun' is included by Erasmus in his *Adages* II.v.7 (*CWE* 33, 245).

4. *Palinurus ... Plato*: Palinurus, the steersman of Aeneas, was overcome by sleep and fell overboard to his death (*Aeneid* 5.833–71; 6.337–83); in contrast, Ulysses and Plato represent travel seen as the quest for knowledge.

5. *nothing . . . Seneca and Cicero*: More makes the same point again in his 'Letter to Oxford' of 1518, in which he defends the study of Greek against its opponents (*CWM* 15, 143). Both Marcus Tullius Cicero (106–43 BC) and Lucius Annaeus Seneca the Younger (*c*. 4 BC–AD 65) were important transmitters of the Greek philosophical tradition into Latin.

6. *Amerigo Vespucci . . . everywhere*: The travels of the Florentine adventurer Amerigo Vespucci, who gave his name to America, were the focus of a highly effective publicity campaign, sparked off by his *Mundus Novus* of 1503, which achieved twenty-three editions by 1506. Of the four voyages that he claimed to have made to the New World, the first was a hoax, as More seems to be aware since Raphael only goes on 'the latter three'; it was on the fourth voyage (May 1503–June 1504) that twenty-four Portuguese sailors were left in a fort at Cape Frio in Brazil, as Raphael reports. Since he then spent a bit over five years in Utopia, that leaves him about six years to complete his circumnavigation of the globe and meet up with More in Antwerp.

7. *He who has no grave . . . heaven*: The first saying comes from *Pharsalia* (7.819), an epic by the Roman poet Lucan (AD 39–65); the second derives from the Greek philosopher Anaxagoras (*c*. 500–428 BC), as quoted by Cicero in his *Tusculan Disputations* (1.43.104).

8. *Scyllas . . . such-like horrors*: Typical hazards of a traveller's tale: Scylla was a six-headed monster who preyed on passing sailors (*Odyssey* 12.73–100, 234–59; *Aeneid* 3.420–32); Celaenos was one of the malevolent Harpies who combined women's heads with the bodies of birds (*Aeneid* 3.209–58); the Laestrygones were cannibalistic giants (*Odyssey* 10.80–132).

9. *republic*: This seems likely to be the point at which More inserted the section on counselling kings that he wrote after returning to London.

10. *I live as I please*: This formula echoes Cicero's account in *De officiis* (*Of Duties*) of those, like Raphael, who avoid public life to preserve calm of soul; in an early letter the young More applies it to himself (see *Selected Letters*, E. F. Rogers, ed., New Haven: Yale University Press, 1961, p. 2), and the theme recurs in his *Life of Pico*, CWM 1, 85–8.

11. *the rebellion . . . slaughter*: In effect a taxation protest, the Cornish uprising of 1497 was crushed at Blackheath in sight of London; poorly armed, the rebels were cut down, and up to 2,000 were killed.

12. *John Morton . . . Chancellor of England*: John Morton (1420–1500) became Bishop of Ely in 1479, under which title he plays a key part in More's *Richard III*; exiled under Richard III, he rose to the highest offices of Church and State after the accession of Henry VII. More served as a page in his household *c.* 1490–92.

13. *the laws of your country*: In other words the Common Law, peculiar to England.

14. *the French wars*: This must refer to the Anglo-French hostilities of 1489–92, but indirectly it alludes to Henry VIII's grandiose invasion of France in 1513.

15. *just like drones*: To Plato drones, or mere consumers who contribute nothing to the community, are 'the bane of the hive'(*Republic* 552c–d).

16. *wise-fools*: More here adapts the Greek term *morosophoi*, literally 'foolish wise men', which was coined by Lucian (*Alexander* 40) and adopted by Erasmus in *The Praise of Folly* (1509) (*CWE* 27, 88) and elsewhere to mean those who are officially wise but get it wrong.

17. *as Sallust drily puts it*: Sallust (86–35 BC) was a Roman historian; the reference is to *The War with Catiline* 16.3, where he describes Catiline's corruption of his young followers.

18. *the French military . . . your conscripts*: More, who was not above a little jingoism, may be thinking of the Battle of the Spurs (1513), so-called from the speed of the French withdrawal. The case for national rather than mercenary forces is also put by Machiavelli, who cites Henry VIII's campaign, in *The Discourses* (1519), 1, chapter 21.

19. *They leave nothing . . . sheep fold*: In May 1517, just six months after *Utopia* appeared, the government initiated a major inquiry into the negative effects of enclosures.

20. *inappropriate display . . . food and drink*: Sumptuary laws to control consumption, including dress, were a regular feature of English legislation from 1337, including Acts in 1510 and 1515. The aim was to curb extravagance, to clarify social distinctions or 'estates' and to reduce costly imports. The effect was minimal.

21. *this extreme justice . . . injury*: Raphael is here echoing Cicero's dictum, 'More law, less justice' (*De officiis* 1.10.33).

22. *Manlian orders*: The severity of the Roman commander Manlius (4th century BC), who had his son beheaded for a technical infringement, became proverbial, as in Erasmus, *Adages* I.x.87, 'Manlian commands' (*CWE* 32, 274–5).

23. *the Stoic maxim that all crimes are equal*: The Stoics held that all violations of the moral order offended against reason and nature and were thus rated as equally culpable.

24. *the law of Moses ... death*: The Mosaic rules on theft are given in Exodus 22:1–4; death was the penalty for certain other crimes.

25. *banning any right to sanctuary*: The right of criminals to seek refuge in sacred places such as a church was a contentious issue, and had been increasingly restricted in the course of the 15th century.

26. *a Venus*: In antiquity a Venus was the highest throw of dice or knucklebones, cf. Erasmus, *Adages* I.ii.13, 'If you throw often, you'll throw this way and then that' (*CWE* 31, 154–5).

27. *you won't get rid ... friars as well*: The point of the story is that the orders of friars were mendicants, i.e. beggars; unlike monks, who drew their revenues from monastic estates, friars were dependent on charitable donations from the laity.

28. *stung by the vinegar*: An allusion to Horace, *Satires* 1.7.32, 'soused with Italian vinegar'.

29. *a son of perdition*: One doomed to be lost, John 17:12; 2 Thessalonians 2:3.

30. *In your patience ... souls*: Luke 21:19.

31. *Be angry, and sin not*: Psalms 4:4, based on the Latin of the Vulgate text, *Irascimini*, 'Be angry'.

32. *The zeal ... eaten me up*: Psalms 69:9.

33. *Those who mocked . . . baldhead*: The verse comes from a sequence composed for Easter Sunday by Adam of St Victor (*c.* 1110–*c.* 1180) and alludes to the story of the prophet Elisha, who was mocked for his baldness by a group of boys; when he cursed them two bears promptly emerged from the woods and killed them (2 Kings 2:23–4). The zeal in question here is righteous anger against those who mock the sacred.

34. *Answer a fool ... folly*: Proverbs 26:5

35. *how much more . . . baldheads*: Given the grim fate of those who mocked Elisha (see note 33), the implication is that an even worse one awaits those who mock the friars, whose heads have been shaved in a tonsure.

36. *a papal bull ... excommunicated*: The papal bull would be 'Exiit qui seminat' ('He who sows') issued by Nicholas III in 1279.

37. *philosophers rule . . . philosophize*: On the conjunction of power and wisdom, see Plato, *Republic* 473c–d and *Letters* VII, 326a–b.

38. *what he experienced ... Dionysius*: Plato's unsuccessful attempt to convert Dionysius, the tyrant of Syracuse (367–357, 346–344 BC),

to philosophy is described in his *Letter* VII and in Plutarch's *Dion* 4.1–5.3; 10.1–20.2.

39. *Now imagine*: The two imaginary scenes that follow, one at the French court, the other at an unidentified court resembling that of Henry VII, are presented in two huge sentences of 464 and 926 words; the translation attempts to convey something of the cumulative pressure they achieve.

40. *other nations . . . invade*: The proposals that follow relate closely to the international situation after the battle of Marignano on 14 September 1515 when the French under Francis I had routed the Swiss and won back control of Milan with help from Venice.

41. *a prince that they don't trust*: One claimant still surviving was Richard de la Pole, Earl of Suffolk, the 'White Rose', a nephew of Edward IV who had fought against the English at Thérouanne in 1513 and would die among the French casualties at the battle of Pavia in 1525.

42. *He ought therefore to care . . . potential*: Cf. Erasmus, *Adages* II.v.1, 'Sparta is your portion; do your best for her' (*CWE* 33, 237–43), one of the major 'social' adages added to the 1515 edition.

43. *some king*: This discreetly anonymous section is probably aimed at the fiscal policies adopted by Henry VII, vividly described by Thomas Penn in *Winter King* (London: Allen Lane, 2011).

44. *the maxim of Crassus*: Raphael here adapts the words attributed to Crassus in Cicero, *De officiis* 1.8.25.

45. *he can do no wrong*: The axiom 'the king can do no wrong' refers to the principle of sovereign immunity in English law, though here cynically distorted.

46. *the prince's interest . . . rebellion*: Raphael's ironical observations echo Aristotle's account in his *Politics* of the tyrant, in whose interest it is to keep his subjects poor and low-spirited; see 3.13 (1284b2–3) on the spirit of rebellion and more generally 5.10–11 (1310a40–1315b10).

47. *what was meant by Fabricius*: The saying actually derives from Manius Curius Dentatus (Plutarch, *Moralia* 194f), but was widely attributed to Gaius Fabricius Luscinus (fl.*c.* 280 BC), a model of frugality.

48. *that academic mode*: Marginal note: *Scholastic philosophy*, i.e. the formal philosophy of university disputation, which is indifferent to context, in contrast to the 'civil' philosophy advocated by humanists, which adapts to its audience.

49. *in the course of a play . . . Nero*: The Latin tragedy *Octavia*, which was once attributed to Seneca, deals with the abuse of power; its high style provides a jarring contrast to the low-life comedy of Plautus (*c*. 254–184 BC), much as Lucian describes a tragic actor 'wearing the high boot of tragedy on one foot and a sandal on the other' (*How to Write History* 22). The underlying issue is one of decorum, adapting to the context.

50. *the role of a philosopher . . . lies*: Plato, Raphael's favourite philosopher, sees a place for helpful lies, in effect for fiction, as a form of social medicine, see *Republic* 382c–d, 414b–415c, 459c–d.

51. *proclaim . . . in their ears*: Matthew 10:27; Luke 12:3.

52. *some leaden yardstick*: The Lesbian rule, a soft, flexible rule of lead used by builders for curved surfaces; see Erasmus *Adages* I.v.93 (*CWE* 31, 465).

53. *as Mitio says . . . madness*: Terence, *Adelphoe* (*The Brothers*) I.ii.145–7.

54. *Plato in a witty comparison . . . others*: *Republic* 496d–e.

55. *he declined to legislate . . . by all*: According to Diogenes Laertius (3rd century AD), Plato refused to advise on the setting up of Megalopolis for this reason (*Eminent Lives* 3.23); for Plato's views on community of property, see *Laws* 739b–c.

56. *It's just not possible . . . distinctions*: These objections to community of property derive from Aristotle, *Politics* 2.3 (1261b16–38) and 2.5 (1262b36–1263b25); they were later absorbed into scholastic thought by Aquinas (*Summa theologica* 2a–2ae.66.2) and others, and formed the basis for conventional ideas about private ownership in More's time.

BOOK TWO

1. *The island has . . . appearance*: Erasmus claimed that More 'represented the English commonwealth in particular' (*CWE* 7, 23), in which case the fifty-four cities may match its fifty-three counties and London. They are city-states like the Greek *poleis*.

2. *As the sea comes in . . . the city*: Marginal note: *The same as the Thames in England.*

3. *The city is linked . . . hindrance*: Marginal note: *In this London is like Amaurot*; but in London the bridge was at the centre of the town, which was a hindrance to shipping.

4. *No house is without . . . enter*: Marginal note: *This sounds like Plato's community.*

5. *1,760 years . . . island*: That would be since 244 BC, when the
    reforming king Agis IV became King of Sparta.

6. *all the syphogrants, two hundred of them*: So there are 6,000
    families in each city, leaving aside the country granges. It isn't
    clear why Raphael henceforward adopts the older names for the
    various orders of magistrates.

7. *business is never discussed . . . session*: Marginal note: *Would
    that the same happened today in our councils.*

8. *expeditions . . . through play*: Cf. 'If a boy is to be a good farmer
    he should play at farming', Plato, *Laws* 643b–c.

9. *the common fate . . . Utopians*: Tudor regulations allow for eight
    working hours in winter, and in the period from March to Sep-
    tember extend these from 5 a.m. to 8.00 p.m., with two hours
    free.

10. *each household . . . sixteen adults*: With a family average of thir-
    teen adults, this yields some 78,000 in a city, plus children and
    slaves; the numbers on the rural granges are not clear. At the time
    London had about 50,000 inhabitants.

11. *such practices . . . feelings*: Marginal note: *By butchering beasts
    we learn to murder men.* The argument is attributed to Pythago-
    ras (6th century BC) by Ovid (*Metamorphoses* 15.72–142), and
    used by Erasmus in 'War is sweet to the uninitiated', *Adages* IV.i.1
    (*CWE* 35, 407–10). The work is done by 'bondsmen' (*famuli*)
    rather than by slaves (*servi*); this may refer to those outsiders
    who freely opt to serve in Utopia, as distinct from criminals con-
    demned to servitude (see p. 91 above).

12. *each residential block . . . row*: Presumably a square block with
    gardens in the middle, each side of the square consisting of a row
    of thirty houses with the hall at its centre.

13. *They burn spices . . . comes of it*: Burning aromatics became
    customary in aristocratic households by the late 15th century; in
    Utopia all have access to such refinements.

14. *no wine-bars . . . encounters*: Marginal note: *O holy common-
    wealth, worthy to be imitated even by Christians!*

15. *they use the gold . . . homes*: Marginal note: *What splendid con-
    tempt for gold!*

16. *their marbles, their lockets and their dolls*: More probably took
    these emblems of childhood from the *Satires* of the Roman
    author Persius (AD 34–62): for marbles see 1:10; for lockets,
    5:31; for dolls, 2:70.

17. *what shocks them . . . rich*: Marginal note: *How much wiser are
    the Utopians than the mass of Christians!*

18. *Parva logicalia*: The 'little logic' by the scholastic Peter of Spain (13th century), so-called according to More 'because it contains little logic'; it was the basic textbook for the university arts course. On the technical terms given by More, see *CWM* 15, liii–lv.

19. *second intentions . . . 'man-in-general'*: 'Second intentions' are purely intellectual conceptions that derive from 'primary intentions' or the mind's direct apprehension of an object; the Utopians, it is implied, are too down-to-earth to grasp such abstractions as 'man-in-general'.

20. *the goods of the mind . . . to the mind*: Plato distinguishes different types of goods, i.e. good properties: goods of the soul, such as temperance; goods of the body, such as health; and external goods such as wealth or status (*Laws* 697b). The distinction is adopted by Aristotle, *Politics* 7.1.3–4 (1323a24–1324a3); *Nicomachean Ethics* 1.8.2 (1098b12–22). That the Utopians parallel the Greeks suggests the universality of natural wisdom.

21. *their paramount concern . . . happiness*: Their position is close to that of Epicurus (341–270 BC), whose austere doctrine of pleasure was revived in the Renaissance; they differ however in 'certain principles drawn from religion', that is the immortality of the soul and post-mortem judgment.

22. *the soul is immortal*: Marginal note: *The immortality of the soul, about which these days not a few Christians have doubts.* In fact, it was declared a doctrine of the Church by the Fifth Lateran Council in 1513, but there was debate about whether it could be demonstrated by natural reason.

23. *one dissenting view . . . in virtue itself*: The position of the Stoics, who also saw virtue as living in accord with nature.

24. *either a joyful life . . . to others*: Marginal note: *But today some regard pain as if it were the essence of religion, when really it should be accepted either from natural necessity or as the consequence of some moral duty.*

25. *right reason*: This term refers to the innate faculty of moral judgement or 'common sense' held by many to be planted in human nature.

26. *They consider . . . cruelty*: See note 11 above.

27. *these pleasures . . . discomforts*: Such 'mixed experiences' are discussed by Plato in *Philebus* 46a–d, a work that underlies much of the section on pleasure.

28. *These are their thoughts . . . holier ones*: Marginal note: *Note this point carefully.* More appears to make a distinction here

between the natural reasoning of the Utopians and the Christian transformation of suffering.

29. *provided that there were . . . text*: A typically humanist proviso; cf. More's epigram on Erasmus' correction of the New Testament, *CWM* 3, 2, no. 255.

30. *Theophrastus' treatise On Plants*: Theophrastus (*c.* 372–286 BC) was Aristotle's successor as head of the Lyceum and the effective founder of botany.

31. *Lascaris . . . Dioscorides*: The Greek grammar of Constantine Lascaris (1434–1501) was published in 1476, that of Theodorus Gaza (*c.* 1398–1478) in 1495; Hesychius of Alexandria (*c.* 5th century AD) compiled a Greek lexicon which was printed at Venice in 1514. Dioscorides (1st century AD) wrote a work on medical drugs.

32. *Plutarch's works . . . Lucian*: The *Moralia* and the *Parallel Lives* by Plutarch (*c.* AD 50–120) were highly popular in the Renaissance; More had collaborated with Erasmus in translating works by the satirist Lucian (born *c.* AD 120).

33. *Aristophanes . . . Aldus*: Aristophanes (*c.* 446–386 BC), comic dramatist; Homer, the alleged author of the founding Greek epics the *Iliad* and the *Odyssey* (?8th century BC); Sophocles (*c.* 495–406 BC) and Euripides (*c.* 480–*c.* 406 BC), both celebrated for their tragedies. The press of Aldus Manutius or Manuzio (d. 1515) in Venice pioneered accessible texts of the classics; Erasmus had worked with him there in 1508.

34. *Thucydides . . . Herodian*: Thucydides (*c.* 460–400 BC) and Herodotus (d. *c.* 420 BC) were the major historians of ancient Greece; Herodian (*c.* 170–240) wrote a Greek history of the Roman emperors ruling between 180 and 238.

35. *Tricius Apinatus . . . Galen*: For Tricius Apinatus, see Glossary of Names; Hippocrates (5th century BC) and Galen (AD 129–*c.* 199) were the most celebrated medical writers of antiquity.

36. *philosophy*: i.e. natural philosophy, the forerunner of modern science.

37. *The Utopians don't . . . lands*: This contrasts with practice in the ancient world; in 1503 Isabella of Castile (1451–1504) had banned the enslavement of natives in newly discovered lands, except for those practising cannibalism or resisting conversion. The Utopians only go to war in specific circumstances (see p.99 below), so it would seem that those prisoners they do enslave are fighting against justice. Apart from volunteers from other nations, all their slaves are, in one way or another, moral defaulters rather than social victims; cf. St Augustine, *The City of God* 19.15.

38. *those drawn from among their own people . . . virtue*: A similar policy is proposed in Plato's *Laws* 854e.

39. *a sensible thing to do . . . holy act*: This strictly rational attitude to suicide has classical antecedents, notably in Stoicism, but it clashes with the Christian view voiced by Raphael before Cardinal Morton (see p. 36 above).

40. *choosing marriage partners . . . bride*: This celebrated feature of Utopian life is anticipated by Plato, *Laws* 771e–772a, 925a.

41. *old age . . . fragile trust*: Cf. Erasmus, *Adages* II.vi.37, 'Old age is sickness of itself' (*CWE* 33, 309–10).

42. *no magistrate . . . as such:* The ideal of magistrates as 'fathers' occurs in Sallust's account of early Rome (*Catiline* 6.6) and is taken up by St Augustine (354–430), *The City of God* 19.16.

43. *the governor . . . before him*: In December 1516 More writes to Erasmus, imagining himself as prince of the Utopians, 'crowned with that distinguished diadem of corn-ears, a splendid sight in my Franciscan robe, bearing that venerable sceptre consisting of a sheaf of corn' (*CWE* 4, 163).

44. *Since the well-being . . . interests?*: There is a similarity here, in medieval Italian city-states, to the role of the *podestà*, who was typically drawn from another city and elected by popular mandate. See Quentin Skinner, *Foundations of Modern Political Thought* (Cambridge University Press, 1978), vol. 1, pp. 3–4.

45. *they regard as inglorious . . . war*: This deflation of chivalric values is also elaborated by Erasmus in his adage 'War is sweet to the uninitiated', the most famous anti-war diatribe of the age.

46. *These people . . . reared*: Marginal note: *A people by no means unlike the Swiss*. At the time these were the most effective mercenaries in Europe. Not surprisingly, this note was omitted in the Basel editions of 1518.

47. *seven hundred thousand ducats a year*: The ducat was a gold coin with a value of around four to the English pound; to More's early readers this would have been a staggering sum.

48. *Quaestors*: The magistrates who oversaw public finances in ancient Rome.

49. *they call him . . . native speech*: A Persian deity associated with dawning light, Mithras was widely honoured in the Roman Empire as a sun god.

50. *Christ approved . . . communities*: Marginal note: *Monasteries*; community of property was found among early Christians (e.g. Acts 2:44–5 and 4:32–5) and is fundamental to the monastic life.

51. *the converts had been admitted . . . bishop*: Out of the seven sacraments of Catholic tradition only two, baptism and matrimony, do not require a priest; holy orders are normally conferred by a bishop.

52. *no one should suffer . . . religion*: Utopus' toleration is often contrasted with More's later rigour against heresy; as Lord Chancellor he was under oath to suppress heresy, and he would in any case have distinguished between Utopus' natural religion and the Christian revelation entrusted to the Church.

53. *This belief . . . dishonesty*: The final blow to any hope of privacy in Utopia. In his *Dialogue concerning Heresies* (1529), More sees the saints in a similar role: 'When saints were in this world at liberty and might walk the world about, ween [think] we that in heaven they stand tied to a post?' (*CWM* 6, 213).

54. *'religiosi' . . . 'god-fearing'*: In More's Latin *religiosus* denotes a member of a religious order.

55. *the dignity of the order . . . broadly*: Marginal note: *But what a crowd of them we have!*

56. *they pray . . . either side*: Marginal note: *O priests far holier than our own!*

57. *The priest is clothed . . . value*: A feature drawn from the New World: Pêro Vaz de Caminha (*c.* 1450–1500), who landed with Cabral on the coast of Brazil in 1500, describes feather headdresses and 'a cloth of many colours, also of feathers, a rather beautiful kind of material', C. D. Ley, ed., *Portuguese Voyages, 1498–1663* (London: Phoenix Press, 2000), pp. 52–3. More could have learned of such use of feathers from a variety of sources, including Vespucci.

58. *all things . . . everyone*: Raphael echoes the proverb 'Between friends all things are common', the basis for Erasmus' adage (see Appendix 1). Raphael's references to 'here' and 'there' (in the following sentence), as he talks about Utopia, suggest that he has his worlds mixed up.

59. *a conspiracy . . . commonwealth*: Marginal note: *Reader, note this well.*

60. *She wouldn't even want . . . wealth*: Pride, *superbia* in Latin, is here referred to as a goddess, putting her on the same level as Folly in Erasmus' *Praise of Folly*: both spring from *philautia*, self-love in Greek. For St Augustine pride or self-assertion is the hallmark of the city of this world, as in e.g. *The City of God* 14.13.

61. *I was left with . . . commonwealth*: As in his intervention at the
    close of Book One, 'More' here becomes the mouthpiece for a
    conventional Aristotelian-scholastic view of society in which
    public service is linked to private property and wealth. However,
    the reference to 'popular belief' is ambiguous. Is the real More
    being ironical at the expense of his fictional self?

Acknowledgements

Like anyone approaching More's work today I have benefited from the accumulated experience of past readers, and among the living I am happy to acknowledge a special debt of thanks to Clarence Miller, both as a previous translator and as an encouraging accomplice to my own efforts.

The map and alphabet from the first Froben edition of 1518 are reproduced by permission of the Trustees of the Lambeth Palace Library, and I am particularly grateful to the University of Toronto Press for permission to reprint the adage 'Between friends all is common', from the *Collected Works of Erasmus*, and to Brepols for permission to reprint the passage from Geoffrey Eatough's *Selections from Peter Martyr*.

My personal thanks go to Jessica Harrison at Penguin for her support, and to Claire Péligry, whose meticulous copy-editing has enhanced the book. Finally, I gratefully acknowledge the computer skills of H. C. B-S which prevented the whole enterprise, rather like Lucian's Plato, from vanishing into oblivion.

PENGUIN CLASSICS

THE COMPLETE POEMS
JOHN MILTON

> 'I may assert Eternal Providence
> And justify the ways of God to men'

John Milton was a master of almost every type of verse, from the classical to the religious and from the lyrical to the epic. His early poems include the devotional 'On the Morning of Christ's Nativity', 'Comus', a masque, and the pastoral elegy 'Lycidas'. After Cromwell's death and the dashing of Milton's political hopes, he began composing *Paradise Lost*, which reflects his profound understanding of politics and power. Written when Milton was at the height of his abilities, this great masterpiece fuses the Christian with the classical in its description of the Fall of Man. In *Samson Agonistes*, Milton's last work, the poet draws a parallel with his own life in the hero's struggle to renew his faith in God.

In this edition of the *Complete Poems*, John Leonard draws attention to words coined by Milton and those that have changed their meaning since his time. He also provides full notes to elucidate biblical, classical and historical allusions and has modernized spelling, capitalization and punctuation.

Edited with a preface and notes by John Leonard

PENGUIN CLASSICS

SIDNEY'S 'THE DEFENCE OF POESY' AND SELECTED RENAISSANCE LITERARY CRITICISM

'The poet with that same hand of delight doth draw the mind more effectually than any other art doth'

Out of the intellectual ferment of the English Renaissance came a number of outstanding critical works that sought to define and defend the role of literature in society and to comment on the craft of writing. Foremost among these is Sir Philip Sidney's *The Defence of Poesy*: an eloquent argument for fiction as a means of inspiring its readers to virtuous action. George Puttenham's *The Art of English Poesy* is an entertaining examination of poetry, verse form and rhetoric, while Samuel Daniel's *A Defence of Rhyme* considers the practice of versification and praises the English literary tradition. Along with pieces by such writers as Sir John Harrington, Francis Bacon and Ben Jonson, these works reveal the emergence of new critical ideas and approaches, and celebrate the possibilities of the English language.

Gavin Alexander's introduction sets these writings in the context of the Renaissance and discusses the traditions of humanist literary criticism and rhetoric. This edition also includes detailed notes on each work, further reading, glosses and a chronology.

Edited with an introduction and notes by Gavin Alexander

PENGUIN CLASSICS

THE COMPLETE POEMS
ANDREW MARVELL

'Thus, though we cannot make our sun
Stand still, yet we will make him run'

Member of Parliament, tutor to Oliver Cromwell's ward, satirist and friend of
John Milton, Andrew Marvell was one of the most significant poets of the
seventeenth century. *The Complete Poems* demonstrates his unique skill and
immense diversity, and includes lyrical love-poetry, religious works and biting
satire. From the passionately erotic 'To his Coy Mistress', to the astutely political
Cromwellian poems and the prescient 'Garden' and 'Mower' poems, which
consider humankind's relationship with the environment, these works are
masterpieces of clarity and metaphysical imagery. Eloquent and compelling, they
remain among the most vital and profound works of the era – works by a figure
who, in the words of T. S. Eliot, 'speaks clearly and unequivocally with the voice
of his literary age'.

This edition of Marvell's complete poems is based on a detailed study of the extant
manuscripts, with modern translations provided for Marvell's Greek and Latin
poems. This edition also includes a chronology, further reading, appendices, notes
and indexes of titles and first lines, with a new introduction by Jonathan Bate.

Edited by Elizabeth Story Donno

With an introduction by Jonathan Bate

THE STORY OF PENGUIN CLASSICS

Before 1946 ... 'Classics' are mainly the domain of academics and students; readable editions for everyone else are almost unheard of. This all changes when a little-known classicist, E. V. Rieu, presents Penguin founder Allen Lane with the translation of Homer's *Odyssey* that he has been working on in his spare time.

1946 Penguin Classics debuts with *The Odyssey*, which promptly sells three million copies. Suddenly, classics are no longer for the privileged few.

1950s Rieu, now series editor, turns to professional writers for the best modern, readable translations, including Dorothy L. Sayers's *Inferno* and Robert Graves's unexpurgated *Twelve Caesars*.

1960s The Classics are given the distinctive black covers that have remained a constant throughout the life of the series. Rieu retires in 1964, hailing the Penguin Classics list as 'the greatest educative force of the twentieth century.'

1970s A new generation of translators swells the Penguin Classics ranks, introducing readers of English to classics of world literature from more than twenty languages. The list grows to encompass more history, philosophy, science, religion and politics.

1980s The Penguin American Library launches with titles such as *Uncle Tom's Cabin*, and joins forces with Penguin Classics to provide the most comprehensive library of world literature available from any paperback publisher.

1990s The launch of Penguin Audiobooks brings the classics to a listening audience for the first time, and in 1999 the worldwide launch of the Penguin Classics website extends their reach to the global online community.

The 21st Century Penguin Classics are completely redesigned for the first time in nearly twenty years. This world-famous series now consists of more than 1300 titles, making the widest range of the best books ever written available to millions – and constantly redefining what makes a 'classic'.

The Odyssey continues ...

The best books ever written

PENGUIN 🐧 CLASSICS

SINCE 1946

Find out more at www.penguinclassics.com